Burning Water

Burning Water

a novel by

George Bowering

Cataloging in Publication Data
Bowering, George, 1935-
Burning Water

ISBN 0-8253-0005-3

1. Vancouver, George, 1757-1798 – Fiction.
2. Explorers – Canada – Fiction. 3. British Columbia – Discovery and exploration – English – Fiction. I. Title.

PS8503.092B87 813′.54 C80-094375-9

Cover design/Maureen Henderson

First published in 1980 in the United States by
Beaufort Books, Inc., New York

Printed in Canada First Printing

ISBN 0-8253-00005-3

Acknowledgements

I would like to offer my appreciation of the Canada Council, from which I received an Arts Award that made the eventual writing of this book possible.

Certain chapters, in earlier drafts, were published in the following magazines: *Island; Open Letter; Periodics; The Capilano Review; Writing*.

As well as the obvious passages from the writings of George Vancouver and other officers of his expedition, I have made short quotations from the following books: *Vanity Fair* by William Makepeace Thackeray; *Duino Elegies* by Rainer Maria Rilke; *G.* by John Berger; *Mardi* by Herman Melville; *The Tempest* by William Shakespeare.

I would like to dedicate this book,
if he does not mind, to George Whalley

Prologue

When I was a boy I was the only person I knew who was named George, but I did have the same first name as the king. That made me feel as if current history and self were bound together, from the beginning.

When I came to live in Vancouver, I thought of Vancouver, and so now geography involved my name too, George Vancouver. He might have felt such romance, sailing for a king named George the Third. What could I do but write a book filled with history and myself, about these people and this place?

In the late sixties I was a poet, so I wrote a poetry book about Vancouver and me. Then a radio play about us, and on the air we all became third persons. But I was not satisfied. The story of the greatest navigational voyage of all time was not lyrical, and it was certainly not dramatic. It was narrative. So I began to plan a novel, about us, about the strange fancy that history is given and the strange fact that history is taken. Without a storyteller, George Vancouver is just another dead sailor.

How could I begin to tell such a story? I asked myself. Books do have beginnings, but how arbitrary they can be. In 1792, for instance, some English ships appeared out of the probable fog off the west coast of North America, where Burrard Inlet is now, but in the late sixties of the twentieth century I was staring at the sea from Trieste and composing verse about those European mariners visiting the western claims of British North America.

So of course that book had a lot of myself mixed up in it, though it had to be objective if it was to be any good. It was only because I had put my own eyes into the poem and its story that those rocks and shoals were actual enough to make exploration worthwhile. This is as far as I, George, have come, I ended up saying; but later I wanted to say more, and not from my lyrical self. Get away from Vancouver, I said, and went back to Trieste, as far eastward as you can go in western Europe, among seafaring Europeans or their descendants, to do it for real this time, their story.

It was my idea to move my body a long way from the putative setting of the story, from the western edge of European America to the eastern tail of western Europe, that strip of seaman's coast that everyone at one time has seemed to desire. There was that spill of white mountains and foggy water that Romans and Venetians, Hapsburgs and Fascists had fought for and signed papers for, a backyard whose every square centimetre has been stepped upon by someone in all the generations of the families living there. A block from my hotel was a Roman theatre, across the street from the police station. Men in togas, at least in the summer sunshine, used to stand in the square and feel the sun on their foreheads.

And that same sun shone upon the thousand miles of coast they were all getting ready to fight for and negotiate hundreds of years later, and that sun is still burning. I knew that because the Italian pilot of the

DC-9 took us all up into the bright shine for a moment's steep bank between the fog of Milan and the fog of Trieste.

So we Georges all felt the same sun, yes. We all live in the same world's sea. We cannot tell a story that leaves us outside, and when I say we, I include you. But in order to include you, I feel that I cannot spend these pages saying *I* to a second person. Therefore let us say *he*, and stand together looking at them. We are making a story, after all, as we always have been, standing and speaking together to make up a history, a real historical fiction.

Part One

Bring Forth a Wonder

1

Whatever it was, the vision, came out of the far fog and sailed right into the sunny weather of the inlet. It was June 10, 1792.

It could have been June 20 for all the two men who watched from the shore could care. The shore was rocks and scrubby trees right to the high tide water line. The two men were Indians, and they knew enough to blend in with the rocks and trees, for the time being at least.

"It is the first time in my life that I have seen a vision," said the first Indian.

"A vision?" said the second Indian.

"The old folks told me about them. They said you went alone to the woods with no food for a week or two, and you would see visions. Well, maybe I have not been eating much lately."

The second Indian, who was about ten years older, a world-weary man with scars here and there, sighed.

"You have had no particular problem with eating," he said. "You eat more than I do, though I carry more than you do."

"I am still growing. Surely you would not deny me the nourishment I require to take my place as a full man of the tribe?"

These young ones could be pretty tiresome. Full man of the tribe. Talk talk talk. The second Indian looked over at his companion, who was now leaning back on a bare patch of striped granite, idly picking at his navel. And now he is seeing visions.

"I will make certain that I give you half of my fish tonight, before you start hinting for it this time. Meanwhile I might as well tell you about this vision you are seeing."

The first Indian looked up from his belly as if he had forgotten about the vision. He held his hand up, palm downward, sheltering his eyes as he gazed out over the silver water, where another vision or whatever had joined the first. When it got close enough it would be seen to be larger than the first one. The first Indian put his fishing gear down on a flat rock and climbed a little closer down to the water. Much farther and he would fall in and the second Indian would have to rescue him from drowning for the second time in a week. I am an artist, he had said the first time, what do I know about swimming? To which his lifeguard had replied: or about fishing?

"Okay, what do you see?"

"I see two immense and frighteningly beautiful birds upon the water."

"Birds?"

"Giant birds. They can only be spirits. Their huge shining wings are folded and at rest. I have heard many of the stories about bird visions, the one who cracks your head open and eats your brains . . ."

"Hoxhok."

"And others who alight from the mountains and the skies and take away unsuspecting children and people with bad personalities. Also the one with the hopelessly long name who eats eyeballs. But never anything quite like this."

"Maybe, then, it is a vision that rightly belongs to another people entirely," suggested the second Indian.

"An interesting thought, but the fact is that it has been revealed, in the present case, to *us*."

"Then you do think there is something to facts?"

"Of course. But facts can only lead us to visions. Some of us, at least, were born to see visions."

"That is perhaps why you have so much difficulty getting a fish to leave the sea and come home with you. He is a fact whether he is hidden under the surface, or changing colours on the rocks. To make this fact your fact, you need skill and a well-made hook."

"But a vision is not a fish, my old ironic friend."

"I was perhaps making that very point in its opposite order," said he.

"But look yonder, how the late afternoon sun has picked out the true aspect of those wings at rest. Now they are revealed to be gold, and we are two lucky men to have seen this. We will camp here tonight, and while the visions remain I will watch them . . ."

"You'll be asleep a minute after it gets dark."

"I will watch them until they have flown back into their sky or heaven or homeland up in the air. Then I will open my mind to the Great Spirit, and create a song, and the song will reveal the meaning of the vision, and I will take it back with me to the tribe, where I will be accepted and welcomed as . . ."

"A full man of the tribe."

He stopped writing and went out for a while in the Triestino sunlight. When he came back this all seemed crazy.

"Yes, a full man of the tribe. You should not sneer. That is perhaps more than you think I am, but it is also perhaps more than you feel need of for yourself."

The second Indian spat in the direction of those two giant swans or whatever they were.

"You see those visions of yours?"

"Yes, I see them. Oh, I get it. Very clever. But I do see them and so do you, so that takes care of your precious facts, too."

"Not quite." Now he was going to get the brash little squirrel. Little prick. "Those are boats."

"Haw haw haw!"

"Two large dugouts from another people, as I said."

"Oh sure, dugouts with wings."

"Those wings are made of thick cloth. They catch the wind as we are supposed to catch fish in our nets, and travel far out to sea."

"You are only trying to discredit me."

"No, I am discrediting only your fancy. Your fancy would have the fish leap from the water into your carrying bag. But the imagination, now that is another matter. Your imagination tells you where to drop your hooks."

The first Indian looked from his companion to the contraptions and back again. He turned full around, and looked at the second Indian as suddenly as he could, fishing for a truth perhaps swimming in the shadow of a rock.

"You know, I do not want to believe you, but I find it hard not to. I have been bred to believe you."

"Though you were born to see visions."

The artist turned from his older friend with hurt pride and feigned derision. His friend put his hand on his deerskin-covered shoulder and turned him around.

"They are boats. Your fancy cannot dissemble that much. You must allow your senses to play for your imagination. Now, look at the highest point at the rear of the larger dugout. What do you see there?"

The first Indian looked with his very good eyes.

"It looks like a man."

"Yes?"

"In outlandish clothes. Like no clothes ever seen on this sea. He must be a god, he . . ."

The second Indian squeezed tight on his shoulder.

"That is your fancy speaking. That can be very dangerous for people such as us. You must never believe that you have seen a god when you have seen a man on a large boat."

"You have perhaps seen them before?"

"I have."

"Up close?"

"Closer. The vision is made of wood. Hard, smooth, shiny, painted wood. The figures wear peculiar clothes, all right, and some have hair on their faces. Can you imagine a god with hair on his face?"

"Did you hear them speak?"

"No, my imagination did not take me that close. A friend who did hear one speak a year ago said these people come from far in the south, and they call themselves *Narvaez*."

In Trieste, it was raining most of the time, and he would bump other umbrellas with his own on his way down to the piazza, where he would look out at the fog that had drifted in across the northern end of the Adriatic.

It was his idea, crazed in all likelihood, that if he was going to write a book about that other coast as it was two hundred years ago, he would be advised to move away in space too.

It was a neat-sounding idea, but it didn't hold any water at all. In fact it was probably informed by the malaise that had been responsible for a decade of waiting around for a shape to appear out of the fog.

And while there were certainly some people who cared very much whether George Vancouver came back over the ocean with his maps, there wasn't anyone who cared whether *he* ever showed up in Vancouver with a novel written there or elsewhere.

He had thought he would write the book nine thousand miles east because there the weather would be too poor to promote lying on a beach, the city so dull that one day's walk would take care of the sightseeing, and he didn't know a soul (or body) within a thousand miles, and knew only a close relative of the language. He would be ineluctably driven to the manuscript because there would be no telephone to summon his voice for a lecture in a prison, no mail to petition his name for a young writer's attempt to secure a grant to go and write a novel somewhere else, no pub to call for his anticipation Thursday, his body Friday night, and his aching head all day Saturday. No distractions, he said, meaning partly that *she* couldn't get him to change a light bulb or listen to a dream while he should be, as he habitually put it to himself, sitting down in that chair in that tax write-off study, producing.

2

The name of the larger of the two dragon-bird-visions was H.M.S. *Discovery*, that of the smaller was H.M.S. *Chatham*. Thirteen years earlier, H.M.S. *Discovery* had appeared at Nootka, under the command of the as yet uneaten Captain James Cook. Captain Cook has come down in the British historical imagination as a great seaman and superior Englishman. This is so because he told the Admiralty a lot of wonderful things. On one occasion, after the boats had spent days and days in a large inlet far to the north, he said to young Vancouver, his twenty-one-year-old pre-officer, "You see how far we have proceeded inland? This is clearly the largest river in the New World."

"It looks like an inlet, sir."

"You are inexperienced, George. It is the great river we have been waiting to find."

"Shouldn't we wait a little longer to make sure, sir? I mean to say we have been mistaken before now. We thought the strait between the great island and the mainland might be the way east. We called it the Great Inland Sea, you remember?"

"We will call this Cook's River. It is the northern and westward egress of the lake called Superior. We have knit the waterways of British America."

"Yes, sir. Are you going to travel all the way to the lake, sir?"

"No, we will not unnecessarily imperil the lives of our crew, George. We are a good way north, and winter has a way of visiting early and quickly in the interior reaches of this continent, I have been told."

George looked at the weather. It had a way, on this wooded coast, of appearing as a mist turning into rain, squeezing itself against the steep slopes of fir trees that plunged into the sea. Everything in California had tended toward the circle. Here everything inclined to the triangle, sharp straight lines, tree and cliff, mountain and sea.

"So you will be calling the boats back before they reach the headwaters."

"The headwaters are a thousand miles and more to the east, lad. Remember that."

"Yes, sir."

"Besides which, I will require of the men in those boats that they find the gold mines."

"The gold mines, sir?"

"The southern Nootkas are not only dirty, lad, but they are also devious. You will recall that when we first set anchor at Nootka, they asked us for iron. And though it is usual for the Red Man to barter his gold for our iron, these did not offer any such thing. Do you remember what they offered?"

The young man reacted physically. He looked down at his imperfect fingernails.

"Human hands."

"Quite."

Captain Cook had a look of revulsion upon his face, but was it the revulsion of a trader, perhaps, who has been offered an unacceptable deal?"

"We didn't take them, did we, sir?"

"Certainly not! We are indeed a year or more from Britain, but this is still a civilized British ship, and not some French brigantine. I believe that we showed that to satisfaction in the Sandwiches."

"Of course, sir."

On the Sandwich Islands Vancouver had nearly been killed by a native who did not want to return the boat they had argued about. The native had broken an oar over his back, but the young man had retrieved the boat.

He was, despite his reservation, an eager servant of the naval command. But when H.M.S. *Resolution* had reached as close as it could to the South Pole in 1772, just before it turned again north and westward, fourteen-year-old Vancouver had raced to take up his position in the bow, a young *ne plus ultra*. For years he would harbour the ambition to be the closest mortal to the other pole as well. But his pride in being a useful sailor for the Realm would be even stronger.

"These wily aborigines do not even display their gold when the European is in sight of them. We are expected to be duped by the pieces of wood they wear upon their bodies. That is why the men will search out and discover their mines. The king has been informed that this land abounds with gold and silver, with jewels of all classes. He is not going to be deprived of full claim to this coast and its resources by a few tribes of primitives, no matter how clever they prove."

"Of course, sir," said the young sailor.

He was learning a great deal as the apprentice to Britain's most renowned sea captain. Unless Bligh could rightly claim that honour . . .

Well, then was then and now was now. [And now *is* now, but we're forgetting that for the moment.] Here is the lad become captain himself, and one of the things he will do is to resume Cook's voyage and rename Cook's River. He will have the people in the boats measure the entire thing carefully, and then he will dub it Cook's Inlet.

In New Zealand he had measured an inlet once named Nobody Knows What by James Cook, and redesignated it Somebody Knows What. That was an illustration of the humour that attends pride. The boy who had been farther south than anyone else was a Somebody. How much more galling that would make it when the British made Cook a living saint and let Vancouver know that they could have done without his return.

But he knew himself, the real power behind the sails of this ship, once Cook's. He had, in private, tried it a few times, willed a stronger wind alive, and also the opposite, calmed the sea. He never mentioned this to anyone. But it was enough that he knew.

The *Discovery* was not, for all that, a vision, neither vision nor fancy. She was twenty thousand miles from Falmouth again, and that could be achieved over the years only by a brave fact.

She weighed in the water at three hundred and forty tons when she was commissioned as a sloop of war on New Year's Day, 1790. The suggested context for such commission was the French Revolution, and Capt. George Vancouver always wished that he could be firing grapeshot at a French rig instead of dropping sounding lines into a pacific brine.

She was full-rigged as a schooner, with more guns than you could shake a stick at, all mounted on one deck, ten of them four-pounders, and ten on swivels. She sat in place with five anchors, three of them weighing twenty-one hundred pounds apiece.

Her storerooms were packed with salt beef, salt pork, peas, beer, and sauerkraut. Few sailors got sick aboard this ship. Captain Cook had taught Mr. Vancouver that you might keep the storerooms washed down with vinegar, and periodically smoke them out with a mixture of vinegar and gunpowder, lighting fires between the decks to force convection currents. Rats were difficult to find on Vancouver's ship, they said. But they were there. They were only well disciplined. This one was not theirs.

On April 1, 1791, she made sail for the first time. She would be away in the Pacific for four and a half years. She carried a complement of one hundred and one officers and men.

And this is how long she was: ninety-nine feet and a few inches. Ninety-nine feet and a few inches. There are people who can run that distance in three and a half seconds. The bodies on that ship could not have stood shoulder to shoulder along her beam.

Once he had paced the deck of a B.C. Government ferry on the way across the strait to Nanaimo. He walked beneath the lifeboats of the *Queen of Victoria*. Two lifeboats, hung end to end, were as long as H.M.S. *Discovery*.

Last night in Trieste he had not been able to sleep after hearing the two o'clock bells, and had lain there through accumulating noise till breakfast time. But before that *she* had appeared very realistically in his dream, having somehow got over here already. In the dream she was telling him about real waking life.

That was the idea he needed right there, but it didn't sink in for a while.

All the confusion made him think about the good old days, when the realist novelist just had to describe the setting and introduce into it the main characters. He could have told you a hundred things he had seen in Trieste. For instance the guy with no legs in the rain on the Corso Italia, with his leather peaked hat, and the dainty man in the hound's tooth suit who crossed the street just before he came to him, pretending that was *his* car over there, or he had been mistaken in thinking so.

3

William Blake, in those days, was a printer who did not eat a balanced diet, and consequently, being short in any event, tended toward stoutness.

He's the best example you can think of if you're looking for a poet or artist of the period and you want one who was interested in fact. His books might have been about the gods and shades who came to talk with him in his rude chambers, but how did he present them to the world? He did all that painstaking (and finger-peeling) business with copper and acid and corrosive finitude. In other words, if he was going to reach for a word it had better be the right one, because it was going to be etched in. No weekend sailor, this fellow.

Now he was operating in that small city called London at the end of the eighteenth century. Everybody knew everybody, and yet when they produced satires they took great pains to make sure you readers did not read the real names but you knew who was getting it. And they spent a lot of time, it seems to me, commenting about abstract values they all professed to sharing and accused one another of mishandling. I mean taste, virtue, honesty, modesty, piety, that sort of thing.

So not only poetry but also painting was going that way. Painters were making canvases to surround people with values. A country scene depicting humility might be across the room from a battle scene portraying patriotism. The human being in the middle of the room might feel that he was being clad in a second suit of clothes.

Well, William Blake took all the clothes off again, the first English artist to do so in God knows how many years. He wanted his figures to look like Michelangelo's figures. There is nothing abstract about the human form divine.

It was still the Renaissance, after all.

That is, Blake was saying that everything worth representing can be represented by the human form, created first of all by God. Sometimes some awful things can be represented. King Nebuchadnezzar II, big and naked, on his knees, eyes bulging, a wild grass eater. It never seemed that terrible when they just read about it out of the Bible.

What I'm getting at is obvious, I hope, but the connection that proves everything will here follow.

One time some of William Blake's drawings were brought into the rooms of King George the Third, a monarch who had a reputation for encouraging the arts.

When they were shown to him, he looked as you always look at the works of a new artist. Then he looked again and his royal bearing slipped for good.

"Take them away! Take them away!"

That's exactly what he shouted, and that was it for art for the day.

Given what we know about King George the Third, is it any wonder?

4

He thought that if he crossed the seas eastward and set up in an utterly foreign and rather dull north coast city that he would enter the job without any distraction. Instead, he found that the story was less real than it would have been otherwise, that only the distractions were real and seized upon. The imagination, too, fails. Or it finds it very difficult to find footing where the fancy has sent it sailing.

Besides, he thought he was coming down with something, but as he remarked, how can you tell in a foreign country?

It had been Cook's purpose and responsibility to claim whatever lands he found for the British Crown. Vancouver had no such mission. He was supposed to chart the coast, be friendly but firm with the Spanish, and if he had any time left over, keep an eye open for gold and the Northwest Passage.

But Vancouver loved to jump out of a boat, stride a few paces up the beach, and announce: "I claim this new-found land for his Britannic Majesty in perpetuity, and name it New Norfolk!"

Usually the officers and men stood around fairly alertly, holding flags and oars and looking about for anyone who did not agree.

Vancouver thought about Champlain and de Maisonneuve, who got to climb hills with big crosses and plant Christ in the soil of a new world. He wished that there were some Frenchmen around to fight. It had looked, when they left home, as if there would be another colourful war with the French navy, and a great military career was what he wanted to leave behind for his family.

Instead, they sent him as far away as they could, exploring, serving science.

The only Frenchman around had been Etienne Marchand, that little pecker, in the *Solide*. Marchand had taken one look, had seen no way of getting the beaver from the Russians and the Spanish, and gone on home.

One night when he was having a last glass of wine with Captain Quadra, he bared his ambition.

"It has gotten so that I know just what every inlet is going to look like before we even get into it."

"Yes, I know what you mean," said Quadra.

"Do you? Every once in a while, as we are rounding a headland I hope we will find a French man-of-war, hostile to us."

"More of this California grape?" suggested Quadra.

"I keep fantasizing a ball fired through my rigging."

"Oh, really?"

"Come on, John, you know what I'm talking about. War. Wouldn't you like to have a couple of French schooners on your record?"

Quadra shifted his elegant body. He had been drinking a lot of red wine tonight. It had been the usual splendid dinner but he showed no sign of drunkenness, perhaps a little floridness to the face, a little edge to the banter.

"Frankly—ho ho—I wouldn't really care that much. Other than the fact that I would rather sail the Pacific than throw iron back and forth in some smoky bay, I would have to remain neutral to your question."

"Neutral? Oh yes?" Vancouver allowed a nasty look to cross his visage.

"Oh, there is no question but that if and when my king instructs me to sink Frenchmen, I will sink them. It is just that I was born in Lima, you should remember. I am a European only by virtue of the stories and traditions I always heard from my parents and their friends."

"You are a Spaniard, John."

"I am officially a Spaniard. But I am an American. My first sight of land and sky was American. I knew brown Americans all round me, but the only Frenchmen I ever saw were at diplomatic sideboards. You grew up with the image of a tight channel in the North Atlantic, lots of different people speaking lots of different languages. If you imagine yourself seeing a Frenchman with a weapon and killing that Frenchman before he can kill you, you both may be instrumentalizing national policy, but you are both as well repeating the games you played in childhood."

Vancouver looked into his half-empty glass. He just couldn't drink any more. He did not take a great deal in any case, having troubles with both his innards and his mental imagery.

"There is probably much substance in what you say, John, and you are a good friend. But James Wolfe was a friend of mine, and those bastards killed him."

"He managed to take a few with him, George."

"He died on the ground, on *their* Goddamned ground. He was probably England's greatest military commander, and he died on the ground the French bastards had been shitting on!"

You can see what kind of state he was getting into.

"But try to look at it this way, George. He will have a secure place in history. They will paint pictures of his triumphant death, with his body fully-clothed in the colours of his homeland. They will write great poems and perhaps songs about him. His name will live forever in that land. Have they decided on a name for it yet?"

"The Goddamned ground!"

"You are not listening to me, are you, George?"

"I'm sorry, John. I'm sorry you have seen me this way, I really am. I guess I've been under too much strain lately, and that Goddamn Scotchman doesn't help any, either."

Quadra took the expensive goblet out of Vancouver's hand and put it on a sideboard.

"You're doing your job very well, better than any Englishman has done before, George."

"James Wolfe knew what to do with those fucking Scotchmen. I know what I should do with this one. Goddamned scientists! Do you know I found him puking over the side in the Canaries?"

"George, I am not going to join you in a diatribe against science, scientists, or Scotchmen. I am your friend. You are very important to me, and your battles are my battles. But tonight I think we will just let it be."

"Let be . . ."

"Now I am going to wrap you in your cloak and send you home. Give us a little hug, now."

5

He walked all the way round the Santa Maria del Fiore and thought that it had been standing a few hundred years when Vancouver sailed, that in fact it was a couple of hundred years old when, in 1592, Juan de Fuca, real name Apostolos Valerianos, claimed that he had found north of latitude 48° a vast inland sea.

Michael Lok found him in Venice, without any money, a poor Greek. The Medicis, what there was left of them, Cosimo II the little Austrian, weren't ready to listen to stories of some waterway in the North Pacific lands, of all places, so the Greek was up on his luck again, rolled out the old wooden horse full of gold, silver, and pearls he reported seeing on persons and handicrafts of the north coast savages.

"Can you show me some, Juan?"

"Ah, the vicissitudes of the sea, and the expenses of the spirit seeking to keep Christian body together among the Lombards and Venetians, Jews and Tuscan merchants. I have nary a one left save those in my fancy's eye. But they abound in the creek beds and shallow bays of the Anian Straits."

Vancouver was told that while he was there, drawing his very important charts, he might keep his eye peeled for a nice gold necklace, a ceremonial mask of pearls.

"I have been there, you'll remember, and I believe that Juan de Fuca never reached the water given his name by Meares. The ceremonial masks are frightening and curiously wrought, but they are made of red cedar wood. Around his neck a young man might wear the claws of a bear."

"Mr. Meares reports that the area teems with precious metals, and that the Strait of Juan de Fuca is the disgorgement of a great river having its headwaters about the Great Lake."

"Mr. Meares resembles his master Valerianos in that he is a great liar and in that he did probably never advance north of the warm waters of California."

"You will not likely win the favour of your king and people with such disparagements, Mr. Vancouver. What kind of name is Vancouver, anyway?"

"It is not, at the very least, Greek."

"Mr. Meares was, I'll remind you, at one time a naval commander."

"He was that, good enough, but latterly he was no proper explorer, but an adventurist. The beautiful *Iphigenia* flew Portuguese colours every time a vessel larger than a pea pod showed on the meridian."

"You accuse him of cowardice?"

"Let's say a tasteless choice of colours. Did you hear that he claimed to have purchased Nootka Sound? A few crowns, a few pence, as simple as that. I don't know why I am being conveyed thence. Why not simply commission Mr. Meares to purchase charts of all those leagues of ragged coast?"

"You are reckless, sir."

"Not as reckless as the journals of Mr. ex-Commander Meares, for they reck less of the truth than any you'll find this side of Juan de Fuca, strait or

Greek. Had Meares writ said journals himself rather than hiring a hack, perhaps they might seem at least nautical."

"Captain Vancouver!"

"I hate a botched chart, sir."

"You had better see to your own and leave off correcting another's, then."

"They are, in any case, like everything else once held by Mr. Meares, in the hands of the American, Robert Gray. I will perhaps run across him, at which point I will ask whether we might have a look at the tattoos upon the skins of the British seamen sold to him cheap by John Meares."

"It is very likely that your life will be saved by the distance between you and the Admiralty, Vancouver. If your voice were to be heard too often at Whitehall you might find yourself no more popular in London than are your hated French."

"You are in all likelihood right. While I am standing shank-deep in Red Men's baubles I will remember your admonitions, and seek out the most rational pearl device and retrieve it for our monarch."

6

Well, that's the way he was. He thought and knew that he was the best surveyor around, the best navigator in the world. So he hated a lot of people, as the best often do. He hated fakers, as we have seen. He hated people who were satisfied with sloppy jobs. He hated Frenchmen and all other republicans. Yet he was not all that taken with the king, though he himself was the king, and that was something.

Most of all, on this trip, he hated the scientists. Especially that godforsaken Scotchman. Oh yes, he wasn't very strong on Scotchmen.

The little fucker has the deck cluttered up with his stuff, and he is taking over more and more space every day. First there were those contraptions of wood and glass, through which he was going to advise the captain on longitude! Then there were the plants, bushes and trees and weeds from New Holland, New Zealand, the Sandwiches, the Societies, and now the North Coast. I cannot set anchor but the little porridge-eater is off in one of my boats, having commandeered two of my men, to dig up another obnoxious weed, to make a home for it upon *my* planks, and to sequester yet more canvas to make it a roof from the rain, as if it had never felt the rain in this desert!

The vessel is ninety-nine feet long, and he hopes to cover all of it, I'm certain.

Trying to keep that straight in his mind, he imagined the distance from home plate to first base, add two steps. Or say from the red-checkered line to the end boards, to be more patriotic, i.e. loyal to the power brokers in the east.

He knew he had the ultimate power over Menzies. He just wished he would catch him leaning too far over the side, in the middle of the night, somewhere between islands and mainland.

The question of scientists had been bugging the captain for a long time, and it had started, not counting psychological hang-ups from childhood, with the person and character of Joseph Banks, the botanist; pardon me, *Sir* Jos. Banks. He had been the green-thumbed busybody on Cook's voyage of 1768, and when they got back he had used his well-silked thigh and flashing teeth to have Cook introduced, oh don't you know, to everybody at court and anywhere else a returning hero might want to visit with his stories about the Strait of Anian.

So that when slender young George Vancouver walked aboard for Cook's second voyage, he was privy to a polite but serious battle between sea captain and King's Lord Scientist. Banks arrived at quayside with enough equipment not only to laboratize but also to sink the great southern continent when they located it.

Cook said, "Mr. Banks, you are my long-time friend, and, they tell me, a tolerable man of the sciences. In those capacities you are once again welcome to sail with me."

"I am glad to hear of it, my captain, for the king's

pleasure will then be cognate with that of his most enlightened seaman," replied the smooth veteran of many misunderstandings with laymen. He was the clearest type to be fashioned by the whole British eighteenth century. If a bark is to proceed towards the ends of known observation, why of course, equip it thoroughly with the devices created by a finally enlightened being to measure the encountered and record the heretofore unsuspected.

But this time James Cook had one of his infrequent howevers.

"However," he said, "you will instruct your overtaxed workmen to return the major portion of those articulated machineries to the buildings of enchantment whence they crept forth, for they are not going to encumber this sailing ship."

Then there was a lot of polite shouting, during which Banks reminded Cook that he had made his career in high places, to which the sailor replied that his achievements at the helm in uncharted waters had had some effect upon his later advantages, though he did to be sure allow that Banks had been here most gracious, even helpful, and was despite everything a friend.

Young Vancouver watched all this and listened well, and because of a flaw in his own makeup, could not understand why his captain didn't tell the civilian to go fiddle a goose.

The upshot was that Banks pulled all his equipment off the dock and cancelled his plans to make the trip. He announced loudly that the entire voyage would be wasted.

"I will muse on that when I am lying on the white beach, eating a pineapple," said Cook, in a rare moment of light-hearted badinage.

Here he broke off and spent the day walking around the Tuscan capital. In the afternoon he went to one palace that was supposed to be open but it was closed. Then there was the old palace that was supposed to be closed today, but it was open. He decided to go in.

As usual, going through the rooms upstairs, he found after a while that he was going the opposite way to the sequence described by the guidebook and to the few other tourists, some Japanese, the odd German. So he didn't know quite where he was when he stumbled into a room whose walls were covered with painted sixteenth century maps, over fifty of them surrounding a monumental *mappa mundi* in the centre of the room. The first map he spied, on his right upon entry, displayed a fanciful *Cina* and a fanciful *Giapan*. To the north and to the east, all the way to the top right corner of the painting, stretched a sea called the *Stretto di Annian*.

When he saw this, the guidebook fell from his hand and smacked the echoing marble floor.

The next room was the office of Secretary of the Republic, Niccolò Macchiavelli.

Joseph Banks did not go on any more trips to the Pacific, but he became head of the Royal Society in 1778. He was able to move many other people and objects around the globe. He it was who had the Hawaiian, Toweroo, placed aboard the H.M.S. *Discovery*, to be transported after all these years back to his home island. He it was, too, who got Archibald Menzies appointed to his own old job, as naturalist on the 1792 voyage of the *Discovery*, George Vancouver, captain.

In a letter to the young Scot (that is, he was only three years older than the captain), Banks wrote: "How Captain Vancouver will behave to you is more than I can guess, unless I was to judge by his conduct toward me—which was such as I am not used to receive from one in his station. But as it would be highly imprudent in him to throw any obstacle in the way of your duty, I trust he will have too much good sense to obstruct it."

Sir Joseph Banks may have been pampered at court, but he surely should not have been surprised to see his cautious prediction belied by intrigue, torture, buggery and murder.

7

He was driving somewhere, a straight stretch, it must have been back from the Vancouver airport, what other changes will we see in the next two hundred years, alone, when he saw a lone seagull looking down and from side to side as they will, looking for food and a place to light. He saw this while driving his car at thirty kilometres per hour, and a sheet of intuition fell over him. He felt a pressure of memory. Of his earlier life as a seagull.

He was not a mystic, and he was not a nineteen-year-old college student, so he did not rush to someone's house to expound on the vision or whatever it was and where it fit into his mentor's plan.

But it was very authentic, the apprehension, and soon it went away. It did not change his life in any way.

He woke in the middle of the night, something he almost never did. It was as if someone had reached out and shaken his shoulder. For half a minute he did not move even the smallest muscles, but lay on his right side as always, the bedclothes pulled up to and half covering his ear. In a few moments his eyes could pick out details in the cabin. It was quiet, and he remembered that when he went to bed it was still raining. It had been raining steadily for two days, and this evening it had been raining hard enough to make a lot of noise on deck and glass. Now all he heard was a rope creaking as the ship responded to a wave.

He thought that if he did not move his head or his hand or a knee, he would fall back into sleep. He needed it. The pain in his chest did not often these nights let him sleep at an hour of his choosing.

But he closed his eyes and it didn't work. He opened them again and knew he had to turn his head. There was a figure standing at the foot of his bed.

His skin crept cold up his ribs. But he did not move. Who was this who had moved so quietly into his room? He knew that he must not speak first.

The figure was totally silent. He did not move. He was wearing a large sleeping blanket held around his shoulders. He looked at the figure as silent and unmoving now as he, waiting for something he did not desire to start.

At length the ship took a little jig. A beam of moonlight cut across the cabin and illuminated the face that remained still but curious. The eyes were looking at him with a calm desire to see.

He screamed. He heard screams before he could locate them in his own throat. Even then he screamed again, and again, he continued screaming, to get it out, to get it completely out.

There were several men in the chamber, holding him still, holding themselves against him and waiting for him to stop yelling. Women would have shushed and crooned, but these men were quiet, using their bodies to make him fall relaxed, or subdued.

At last he was able to sit without restraint upon the chair fixed to the bulkhead. Some of the men departed, but two remained. They were obviously waiting, for whatever it was to be ended, however it would be, over.

He began, difficult as it was to speak through his broken breath, to tell what he had seen.

But then he stopped. He would not tell them. He would wait for them to go.

The face he had seen had been his own face, looking down at him curiously, his own face.

8

George Vancouver sat at his desk, the dull light from the windows lying soft upon his thick hands, his double chin and puffy cheeks, and on his soft mouth. His short wig was a little crooked. He did not feel well, his stomach was acting up again. It was crazy for a person with his stomach to be at sea all the time, but there he was.

He was writing in his notebook about the totem poles he could see at that moment. They were standing in the dull light in front of the Indians' long houses. He referred to them as "large logs of timber, representing a gigantic human form, with strange and uncommonly distorted features."

He had employed such a description in conversation yesterday with Menzies. The little Scotchman, of course, took the opportunity to start an argument.

"For a person who has gained some fame for speaking to sundry natives in their own languages, you exhibit a remarkable lack of imagination on this occasion," said he, never stopping his fingers from their busy work among his specimens.

Vancouver would have liked to grasp them up one by one and throw them as far as he could over the rail. He could imagine them splashing into the deep green water. Now that was a piece of imagination he was happy with.

"Language is one thing, sir, and whittling is something again," he said. "Learning a naked foreigner's tongue is the first step in creating some form of government. Without the language we would never have brought peace among the kings of the Sandwiches."

"Agreed. You have a wonderful lack of shyness when it comes to the unusual lingo, especially the voices never dreamed of by the phrasebook makers in Europe."

"But carving and daubing trees is not a useful pursuit in the affairs and government of men, and I will not waste my time upon them. We are not here upon the grand tour."

Mr. Menzies' fingers plucked and dug among the ferns. Vancouver would have enjoyed attempting a kick of one over the taffrail, but they were destined, many of them, for the king's garden at Kew.

"I cannot help thinking that languages have purposes beyond allowing one man to tell the other his demands upon his behaviour. There is song, for instance, my captain."

"Well, sing, Menzies. By all means, sing."

"There is also, I venture, a language that is neither spoken nor writ."

Vancouver straightened himself impatiently. He detested the supercilious tone of the other, but it was not a great enough thing to punish the man for.

"A language that is neither spoken nor writ is a language neither heard nor read, and therefore a failure at the principal task of any language, that is to communicate information from one person to another," he said.

"Then in this case, if the poles are a language, and if they have not communicated to you, sir, there is by all means such a failure. But I do not leap to the conclusion you offer, that the failure lies in the expression of the language."

The captain's puffy face turned red.

"You are going to lexicon for me this language, sir. I cannot fail but suspect that this is the direction of your discourse."

"I would begin," said the botanist, coolly, "with your notion that they are giant human figures distorted. In my observation, each of the figures is made of a succession of figures, whale, bear, beaver perhaps, man, great bird, and others. No two houses have a like order of beasts on their poles. Does that, in the matter of communication, begin to tell us something?"

Vancouver walked a few paces away. Then he stopped, and asked one of his infrequent questions of the man he liked littlest on his vessel.

"What about you, scientist? Do the painted poles speak to you?"

"Oh, everything in nature has something to tell me," said the little botanist, fingers still busy as if making messages in the soil around the greenery.

9

When he left Florence he left the warm sunshine behind him, and sailed, or rather entrained, north into the familiar mist and damp threat of rain. He would have to dig his umbrella out again.

Not that it did not rain a lot at home, or where he came from. Of course it did, his home was famous all over the country for being rainy. But here he was an ocean and a continent away, and one could expect something at least novel. To tell the truth, it *was* different. It was lonelier alone in the damp.

"Il faut savoir que tout rime."

It was not that Vancouver did not love anyone. He felt often his absence from his sisters and his brother John. John had directed his first steps to sea. He felt something like love for James Cook, though he had certain difficulties with Cook's vanity and ambition. Since the age of fourteen he had looked to Captain Cook as his chief and best teacher. Cook was the most progressive and intelligent sea captain in Britain's service. When he died his body could not of course be returned to its homeland, but his reputation and his exploits, his gift of years to the grateful Admiralty, would be paramount in naval history.

So George Vancouver loved his memory. Or at least he held the greatest respect it would be possible to hold.

He also loved his ship, and he felt very fatherly or something like that toward his officers and crew. He was only thirty-five, but he knew that many under his command thought of him naturally as older. He took care of his charges better than did any other captain at sea, under any flag. He was carrying on the presence of *his* father, James Cook.

When he encountered a seaman hauling in some rope somewhere, he would probably say, "Good job, lad, keep up the good work."

Or when he met a native chief he had not talked with for a year, he was sure to ask, "Is your family thriving? Good, good."

Once he had said this to a minor chief whose wife had been eaten by a major chief a month earlier. Such was Vancouver's diplomatic skill that he and his people had made it back to the ship without a ruckus, though they were not, to be sure, invited for dinner.

So, if he could get along so well with people whether they were wearing pigtails or birchbark skirts, why was he having all this trouble with Archibald Menzies?

The little Scot was a gentle and quiet enough man. He generally did his job, and did it well, and most of the time he managed to stay out of one's way. Vancouver was prepared to admit that much.

But there was something. When the captain encountered the botanist at work, either aboard ship or on the mossy earth, he naturally uttered a passing remark, or a "how d'ye do" perhaps, or more often a few words about the doctor's work.

And almost every time this occurred, the little

Scotch botanist would continue at his digging or probing or sketching or scribbling, silently for a while, and then continuing while he replied belatedly to his principal officer's offering.

Every time this happened, Captain Vancouver wanted to swing his sword sideways through the man's hat from behind. He wanted to undo his flies and piss in the pot of one of those precious ferns. He wanted to set sail and "absent-mindedly" leave his tormenter gawking at a berry bush on some infrequently visited island.

He wanted to take Menzies' finest pineapple, and . . .

"Carry on," he would hear himself saying, like some army major.

10

Later in his cabin he was relaxed enough to be disturbed by his earlier thoughts of abandoning Menzies. He remembered his first voyage out, on the *Resolution*. They had been probing at the ice, nosing between floating ice mountains, being enveloped by sudden freezing mists. Cook knew there was a continent there—he had wagered his reputation that the icebergs were fresh water, and he had been proven right again, and they had found something worth drinking from their frigid enemy.

The boy was officially the charge of Mr. Wales, the astronomer, but he put his hand to every task on board ship. He climbed the rigging in the middle of high winds blowing off the ice pack. He pulled a frozen canvas with frozen fingers. He spent hours chipping solid ice off a block so that he could move an ice-coated rope a few more inches through its arc.

One day Mr. Wales and Mr. Foster, the eventual botanist of the *Resolution*, went out in a boat to record some temperatures in the water and on the ice. When they set out it was a brooding grey day in late spring, but within the hour a snap fog closed around every object near the pole. The people of the *Resolution* and the *Adventure* were the only men south of the Antarctic Circle. They were the only people who had ever been south of the Circle. If those two men in the boat were going to return to England, they would have to be found today, by this ship.

Luckily those entirely isolated scientists stayed exactly where they had been working, and luckily the *Adventure* found them early in the evening. When Mr. Wales and Mr. Foster stepped over the rail of their own ship they were immediately wrapped in blankets and escorted below, but young Vancouver, *ne plus ultra*, was there to look sharp into their faces. The eyes of those two men were not shining with relief and jubilation. They looked like the eyes of souls who have witnessed the final judgement.

Surely Captain Cook could be understood. He marshalled discipline and diet to get his command within sight, within touch of that southern soil. But would his resolution take him through temporary breaks in the ice, to the very pole? There were those aboard who did not assume so, but whose doubt did not preclude it. The fifteen-year-old sailor cadet was one of those. He stood and admired, and knew what he wanted to be.

So of course he could not be satisfied with his fantasy about marooning his own botanist. The fancy was a breaking of his own discipline, and he would punish it. That night he slept on the taffrail, and there were watchmen who wondered why. But they were Christians, and older seamen, and they were familiar with the odd ways of their superior officer. They also knew that they were healthy, and that if they'd been out with any other commander this long they would by now have the rotting gums and balding heads of scurvy.

The next day Vancouver struggled with aching

joints and a chest that felt as if someone were sitting on it. But he felt unusually light of spirit.

"How are you enjoying the work, sailor?"

"When it's not a-raining, I could sing to my labours the whole long day, sir," was that worthy's reply.

"That's what I was born to hear," said his captain and it may have been so.

He had never seen James Cook pull such a stunt as sleeping out of doors on purpose, but he knew that he was applying an absolute Dutchman's finish to Cook's spirit. When he was not yet fifteen years old he had seen two of Cook's older sailors begin their long voyage by being flogged for refusing to eat their sauerkraut and carrot jam.

A Grub Street poet would have doubly enjoyed the spectacle in rhyming couplets in the next Saturday's paper, but those two men came home without the scurvy and so did the ship's company that had been enjoined to watch the punishment. As soon as those men were cut down they were handed soft rags for their wounds and bowls of pickled cabbage for their innards.

Thus was Cook's ship run—every detail of a day's progress clearly disciplined, and every order traceable finally to the well-being of the people who worked the vessel through the sea.

The youth learned many lessons on the *Resolution*, but this he learned above all: tight discipline for their sake, and first of all, self-discipline.

His favourite image was one that did not reproduce something he had himself seen, but which was constructed from the reports of men under Cook's command: the English captain methodically surveying the St. Lawrence River, with French guns trained on him from both banks. Thus the loyal impatience hid beneath his systematic charting of this vastly complicated coastline. If only those bizarre carven poles between the forest and the sea were republican cannon. If only he weren't a continent away from those curly-wigged frog-eaters.

Cook was the greatest sea-captain of the century, till now, and the century was nearly out. And his father was a hog-feeder and a cabbage-cutter in Yorkshire. Vancouver's father wore a good suit of clothing in a Norfolk customs house, and his family had once been the van Coevordens from across the channel.

Thus it was that he must sleep in the fog of night after an unworthy visitation of caprice.

All that same night Archibald Menzies slept in his customary bedclothes, the covers in his hand held to the side of his head, the candle lit beside his last-minute book of physic. He was satisfied to accumulate knowledge. He was an eighteenth century man.

Not for him the necessity and the pride of that youth who was *ne plus ultra* and must now be also *rara avis*.

11

Vancouver might have anticipated his feelings about Menzies. He knew, for instance, that when it came to exploring and trading in British North America, first it had been the French, and then it had been the Scotch. Everyone knew that.

First the French came and assigned their priests to hold the cross over the heads of the Red Men, and then the Scotch came and sent scouts out for the fur agencies, to see where the great western rivers were going to come to a culmination. The Scotch were more in the way of loners.

When Alexander Mackenzie reached Point Menzies in 1793, he discovered that he had missed Vancouver's ships by a month, the latter having departed for the work in the north.

While he was ensconced there, repairing his gear and doing a little fishing, he managed also to do quite a bit of talking with the Coastal Indians. One of them, he found, was a real pain in the neck. This person pressed himself close and aggressively recounted how the chief white man, Macubah, had caused the natives to be fired upon, and how the plant man, Bensins, had struck him across the back with the flat side of his sword.

"You were fortunate that he was a level-headed Scottish scientist," said Mackenzie.

"Eeyuh, eeyuh. Maybe Baxbakqualanuxiwae will eat him up in the northern forest."

"Oh, I doubt it," said Mackenzie. "If the volcanoes in the Sandwiches didn't get him, no long-named Anian ghost will, either."

It was too bad that Mackenzie did not get there a month earlier. Having rafted right down to the Arctic seas, he could have told Vancouver there wasn't any Northwest Passage this side of the ice.

Vancouver more than half suspected that, anyway. With Cook he had travelled as far north as the western coast of New Norfolk, and had settled for Cook's River. Vancouver had suspected the inlet all along to be the brassy hope of a sea captain who knew he probably wouldn't be back this way.

But he had to respect Cook. The others never had the nerve or the discipline or the imagination of a James Cook. So in his log for All Fool's Day, Vancouver tells us that he has to laugh out loud when he thinks of the "closet surveyors" behind desks in Plymouth and London, constantly "discovering" the great waterway from the Chinese trade in the Pacific to the Great Lake and the St. Lawrence River.

In addition there is an untowardly ribald passage that does not warrant quoting at its length, but which might be summarized. It involves Juan de Fuca, John Meares, and Miguel Fuentes (all of whom stopped somewhere south of their claims) with their pants down, noses in one another's apertures, saying, "I've found the Northwest Passage," and "No, here is the Strait of Anian!" and the like.

A rather fanciful and comical picture for all its

unacceptable coarseness. It shows that George Vancouver, despite his indifferent health, was not always a severely straightlaced man.

Upon first meeting him, men were prepared for a humourless encounter and association. There was his reputation for discipline that preceded him, of course, but there was also his appearance, which he no doubt traded on. He had a thick and large-featured face, extremely heavy shoulders, so that he gave the appearance of a uniformed bulldog, a neck short enough to be doubted, and an aggressive jaw. He used all of these features in argument, and was never shy about getting into a dispute when he felt that he knew his ground, and he generally felt that way.

From the moment of embarkation Dr. Menzies watched the captain carefully. In doing so he was exercising his scientific and medical curiosity, something one might as well entertain if one is going to be stuck aboard a ninety-nine-foot sloop for a period of years. One look told him that the man was not encouragingly healthy when they set sail, and they were headed, so he had been told, to a part of the globe where the rains never ceased.

His behaviour was not as predictable as he would desire that you thought, either. At Tenerife on the way out, a bunch of Spanish sailors and a bunch of British sailors met in one of those frays that simultaneously display the universal deportment of sailors ashore and represent in the farthest westward land of Europe the international Atlantic tensions that pertained at the end of the eighteenth century.

Seamen were banged on the head, cut with blades, hit with wooden objects, and thrown into the sea. One of the men thrown into the sea was Captain Vancouver, who lost no time in making a complaint at official Island quarters.

But Menzies noted and reported two facts (which, remember, Vancouver loved so fairly) about the fighting: that the English started the violence, and that when thrown into the drink by the Spaniards, Vancouver was in mufti, just a rather stocky man in his thirties.

Menzies not only noted these facts, but he noted them in his log, along with a medical man's observations on the physical condition and mental well-being of the chief officer. It was that scribbling that was to get him into all his later trouble.

12

A few days later he went to Venice and rode a vaporetto from one end of the line to the other. He sat in the bow exposed to the cold sea wind. At the Lido stop he got off and walked the length of the concourse and stood for an hour, entirely alone on the beach, looking out to where the grey sky joined with the grey Adriatic a few hundred yards away.

Then he turned around and took the boat back. A phrase he had memorized went through his lonely head. *Mi mostri la barca di salvataggio, per favore.*

Vancouver's health had not always been as bad as it was on this voyage. In fact when he was in his twenties he used the dietary tricks Cook had taught him in order to rise fast in the ranks of ailing officers. Watching him at work on his home-made beer, a fellow lieutenant would ask, "What are you up to now, then?"

"I am a humble sailor at prayer," was the answer.

So in 1780 he stood with rosy cheeks aboard the *Martin*, pursuing French trade ships around the North

Atlantic, the graveyard of unaccommodating stomachs. Two years later, when the *Martin* was redirected to patrol the Caribbean, her crew had much changed. Once there, he was instructed to assume duties as gunnery lieutenant aboard H.M.S. *Fame*, whose crew was perishing from yellow fever. By 1787, in the same sea, he had survived while most around him had been buried there or shipped horizontal to Britain. Due to his miraculous health, his unusual skill in surveying among the thousands of Caribbean islands, and the patronage of Sir Alan Gardner, he became first lieutenant of H.M.S. *Europa*.

He just kept moving into the positions of men who fell ill, and filling them better than his predecessors had. He was a good officer, and was recognized as such by his superiors. But he was never popular. He did not have the social gift, as Cook had had.

Vancouver would be spending his liberty cooking up a big supply of sauerkraut.

"Jesus, that stuff stinks! Why are you making that poison?" another young lieutenant would ask, not with a pleasant tone of voice.

Vancouver would keep on stirring, and see to the heat of the fire.

"I am making my religious preparation for the coming voyage."

"This is no incense you burn at altar."

Vancouver lifted a twig and prepared to cast it upon the flames.

"This is a candle I light to my saint."

Vancouver took a little taste of the boiling cabbage, and a sniff of the vinegar.

"This is the Communion I celebrate in the true expectation that I will be safe in the companionship of the facts," he said.

"Well, y'er a daft one, you are," his associate summed up. "While you are supping on your pickled cabbage leaves and spruce-needle beer, I'll be filling my English gut with salt beef and rum."

"And I were a wagering man, I would lay a groat or two that my teeth will be the tighter when we again see Falmouth."

"I doubt that you'll even see Falmouth again. If your outlandish diet does not kill you, I expect that some night while the black savages' drums are speaking out of the trees on one of the French islands, your own men will hang you for a witch."

"I wouldn't fancy that," said Vancouver. But he kept stirring his odoriferous pot.

13

The relationship between Captain George Vancouver and, well, Don Juan Francisco de la Bodega y Quadra, should have been a simple one, and would have been if the world of politics were as straightforward as Vancouver imagined it to be. I.e., Vancouver arrives at Nootka and formally takes back the landing that the Spanish had so easily taken from John Meares. The treaty had been signed in Europe, and there would be no more fighting. The Pacific was to be Spanish and Catholic as far north as San Francisco. North of that it was not to be Spanish. A bit of a comedown for the Spanish king and navy, and the contradiction of a pope, but nobody wanted to fight that much, and all parties were comfortably convinced to accept the compromise.

That is how simple it was in the eyes of Captain Vancouver, R.N. He loved the simple, the neat, the straightforward. That was why he was sharply honed for the navigation and charting of this serrated coast. For him the simple was the same as the beautiful. But the twisty edge of the North Pacific was a fact. The most exercisable beauty of all was the ability to trace that coast true, representing it as no more even and no more odd than it was. The sea does not do either, and the seaman who belongs on that sea does not do different.

A lot of people wouldn't understand that. The parlour navigators in Westminister wouldn't understand it. John Meares gave ample evidence that he did not understand it. James Cook understood it and lived it till that day of exhaustion in the far northern sea.

But it was not as simple as George Vancouver wanted it to be, of course. One of the reasons was that the Spanish were not Englishmen, and another was that even with that fact recognized, Senor Quadra was not "the Spanish."

In fact he was no more the Spanish than Vancouver was the British, but also no less. His career was fashioned upon his personality in much the same way as Vancouver's. He was fifteen years older than the Englishman, hence his high rank, but he had got to where he was the way Vancouver had, by thriving where others perished, and by watching to see what limits of endurance and bravery and service the older men pushed themselves to, and stepping beyond them.

Seventeen years earlier he had sailed farther north than any other Spaniard would go.

So that when Vancouver came to control the north he knew that he had been farther into Quadra's south than anyone else, and Don Juan was no stranger to the Englishman's northern preserve. They faced one another knowing that neither was going to be able to fake any magic over the other.

Still, Quadra was fifteen years older than Vancouver, and he was the naval commander of the coast. Vancouver was proud of himself but he instantly recognized the pride and the discipline in the Peruvian. He would love to put his ship beside the *Activa*, and sail with the man on a mission to pummel any French vessels they could discover.

Vancouver went often to the *Activa*, taking many meals aboard the Spanish ship while it was undergoing alterations. The English captain, though he easily plunged into chatter with brown royalty on any island in the Pacific, could not dare pretend any of the elegant commander's language, so he brought along a mate from the *Daedalus* to act as translator. Whether or not he had English, Senor Don Quadra let it go at that.

How Quadra the Catholic loved to entertain lavishly, and how purely the Protestant Dutchman returned the favour with simple fare simply provided. Quadra's ship was outfitted in such fashion that when George was there to eat, hundreds of silver plates gleamed in the candlelight, and no one seemed to be counting the gold cutlery.

Vancouver pretended that it meant nothing to him. If the Spaniard wished to serve him champagne wine in crystal goblets, fine. If he chose rather to provide mineral spring water in wooden cups, equally acceptable. Whichever, whichever. But he really loved it. When he returned to the *Discovery*, he said to the watch, "You have a nice dry night for it, sailor." But when he got to his quarters, he did a little skip.

He was a Puritan on the very edge of the world. A sentence spoken in Basel gains no ear around Cape Flattery.

They met on August 28th, 1792, when Vancouver brought the *Discovery* into Friendly Cove. Vancouver fired thirteen guns in respect to the Spanish colours, and the *Activa* replied smartly in kind. Standing in the smoke in his best uniform, polished, brushed, perfectly fitted, among officers equally trim, Vancouver was surprised to hear Menzies' question.

"Haven't we appended a measure of artifice and

ceremony to the sure reliance upon fact and skill?"

Vancouver did not defend himself.

"Don't slouch," he said. "Try to show our hosts that a Scotchman can be taught the rudiments of social behaviour."

"You are addressing a civilian, my shiny friend. And patient."

"While engaged upon this project, you are conjoined to serve orders given by me. I'm not asking you to stand to military attention, though that is what a fair and decent person would do at least. I am simply asking you to stand straight and not lean over the rail. If you don't mind, doctor."

This time Menzies decided to humour the man whose friendship he would have liked to have, but for which he would not grovel. Vancouver understood that and gave the impression that such grovelling would have produced the opposite effect in any case.

The ceremonies ashore were a great success. Everyone was greatly impressed by the show of European manners after all those months of comments and orders mumbled because they were the same each day, and on the most diverting of occasions, grunts and cackles with native women on the warm southern islands.

Being upstairs, of all things, in the great hall of the commander's residence at Nootka was somehow like visiting the model for a marble palace in Madrid or Venice, and not next door to an old Nootka oyster shell dump.

14

In Trieste there was no mail. Vancouver, B.C., was proceeding day by day independent of his help or even knowledge. Was his wife alive? Was his daughter? Did his house stand?

James Cook spent his time at home with Mrs. Cook and their three sons, an excellent salary and praise every day in the Gazette. After his strange and distant death there was a family as well as a nation to mourn him, publicly and in the dark hours after windows went dim along the street.

Who would have remembered longer than the news if George Vancouver had been cooked and eaten somewhere in the other hemisphere? This moment he could quietly slip his legs over the side and let his body fall into the retreating tide, and the world of affairs or the parlours of Albion would never notice the splash.

Even that wouldn't make much of a story.

He wanted to be a famous story very much, the kind of story that is known before you read it. He wanted his name and exploits to be a part of the world any Englishman would walk through.

So he wrote all over the globe. He laid the names of his officers on mountains at north 50° and south 40°. That was a kind of love. He put the names of his sisters on New Albion. He inscribed the names of every officer he had ever respected or needed up and down the coast. But most of all he loved to give abstract names to coves and headlands and passages. They would perhaps write his feelings, so seldom displayed any other way, all over the long-living geography of the southwestern half of the world. Being aboard the *Discovery* probably helped him decide upon Port Discovery, as well as Port Conclusion, Port Decision, Cape Quietude, Hesitation Harbour, The Strait of Inconsistency. He never wrote down on his charts any names that were there before he got there. He didn't imagine that one should.

"And certainly (for novelists have the privilege of knowing everything) he thought a greal deal about" readers far in the future, as far as London and Lisbon, about what they would read when they uncovered his charts. They would read the depth of water, the true configuration of the shoreline, and the name that pressed through his exact head at the exact time that he was required to set ink to surface.

If they did not love him they would not be able to avoid him.

He had even allowed his own name to be affixed to a rock in the antipodes and a mountain in New Norfolk, as far from the common eye as possible, of a certainty.

The king's agents were offering twenty thousand pounds to the man who found the Northwest Passage. He could name it what he liked. Vancouver sailed north and into Cook's River, still convinced that it was an inlet. It was a frightening place to go to prove a disappointment. The tides were running thirty-five feet. The *Discovery* was being banged by large pieces of drifting ice. When she was being moored a quick sea roared up the passage and dumped more than half her supplies into the sea.

Vancouver decided that he would come back and try again, and then he decided that it had better be done now. No one knew whether he would be alive next season. He sent out a last boat company. They did not come back that night. They were not seen the next night. Vancouver wondered whether he should send out another crew to find them or their remains. He remembered the boiled pieces of Englishmen in the pots in New Zealand.

He looked at his crew and only one pair of eyes was looking back, Menzies' of course. No, he could not send them out, not yet anyway. Not *yet?* he thought. It was already questionable whether they would get past the ice to the open sea. Two days later the boat crew returned, cold and hungry and too near expiration to be angry. They said they had attained the farthest point of the southern arm, where a high narrow falls dropped into the salt. No de Fonté's pass. Vancouver himself wrapped his body in a blanket and got into the boat for the first time that year to check out the northern arm with his own faculties. All he found was some Russians.

This is what Vancouver had to say about the former Cook's River: "If Cook had dedicated one more day to its further examination, he would have spared the theoretical navigators the task of ingeniously ascribing to this arm of the ocean a channel, through which a Northwest passage existing according to their doctrines, might ultimately be discovered."

That night Vancouver was very quiet at dinner. He sat in his blanket and coughed from time to time. The younger officers did not say a word or move in their chairs when Vancouver picked up the bowl that held his sauerkraut and carried it with him through a banging door to the deck, and threw it as far as his weakened body would permit.

15

He kept sitting down in a *trattoria* at 7:30 and eating *salsicce con krauti*. He had never eaten so much *krauti* in such a short period. He told himself it was to remind himself that he was holed up in the old Hapsburg seaport.

He couldn't help reflecting a few hours later that a good deal of his book was concerned with eating. What to eat to stay healthy at sea. The way they eat on Spanish ships and the way they eat on Protestant ships. The predilection of savages north and south for eating other people, preferably British sailors and officers. And so on.

Of course he was using more time of his day than was his general custom in thinking about, planning for, searching out, ordering, devouring, and reflecting upon meals. And like certain of his fat friends, he noticed that he was beginning, shortly after the one meal, to think of planning the next. When one is a continent and an ocean from one's own refrigerator one uses a thing like eating to fill one's time.

So: art and life again. Or at least life and

literature. Or if not granting that, fact and imagination. The fancy will not feed your belly—it cannot cheat so well.

The morning after Quadra's big welcome at Nootka, Vancouver had the Spanish leader and his aides to the *Discovery* for breakfast. The fare was a good deal simpler than it had been at the great hall the evening before, but it was distributed with a measure more of ceremony than was usual mornings aboard the British sloop. Gransell the cook really earned his penny that day—he made biscuits of a curious design meant to imitate the eared cactus of Mexico. The drippings were plentiful and uncommonly hot, and there were pineapples kept in the dark all the way from Kauai.

Vancouver fretted because though he had set sail with two dozen of fine ivory-handled table knives, there were now only twenty-three. Puget and Whidbey were surreptitiously sharing one, but Vancouver had been so well impressed by Quadra's board the night before, he was certain that the gentleman had a most meticulous eye for detail.

Well, hang it, we do have a missing blade, and what of it? His Majesty's work consists of something more pressing than the counting of table cutlery.

Then what of the loud commotion that attended the loss of the knife on the island of Hawaii? It could be explained, doubtless, that Vancouver acted most from principle when discipline and its tradition were threatened upon an English vessel for which he had the fact of responsibility.

There were natives, both female and male, of all ages, all over the ship, and the men set to watch for such things had the deuce of a time seeing that the thieving nudists did not strip his majesty's bark down to the superstructure. Luckily the Sandwich Islanders did not wear much in the way of clothes, so they could not, for instance, conceal a full service of plate or a chair beneath robes such as the Patagonians were wont to adorn themselves with.

What the females took away with them when they took their quiet boat ride homewards, only next winter's visit would reveal.

But one evening, just when the orange and red sun was falling into the edge of the ocean like a polychrome postcard, an alarm went up from the galley, and a dark-visaged man raced by the guard and dived with less grace than dispatch into the darkening brine. He just missed two canoes on entry, and was halfway to shore on egress from the water.

"That thief has five of our best *coltelli*," hollered Mr. Gransell, who was under the impression that he had uttered a French plural, and thought that the occasional such borrowing gave class to his galley.

"Hang it, the Old Man will be hotter than last night's fireworks," said the watchman.

"I am already heated fair to well," said Captain Vancouver, who had hied himself to the position upon first hearing the cook's shouts. He had been a bundle of nerves all day, and now he was glad that some action seemed called for.

"You'll be wanting the cutter, sir?" suggested the sailor, anxious to deflect attention from his inevitable failure.

"Of course, we shall employ our one cutter to retrieve our other five," said Vancouver, flushing with excitement and anger in the red light.

"Droll," said Menzies.

"Get fucked."

"No, I mean it," said Menzies, taking his pipe in his hand and looking for all the world like an approving university professor.

"It is time those light-fingered coconut bashers were taught a lesson in civilized European law," said the captain as he stood in the stern of the cutter and prepared to bring Old Bailey to another tropic isle.

Now the king of the island of Hawaii happened to owe Vancouver a few favours, because the white man had brought the animals that started the cattle herds and flocks on the island, and also because just the night before he had provided the most splendid display of fireworks ever seen this side of China.

So it was not long until the king's bodyguard managed to bring the miscreant to the torchlit outdoor after-hours court of criminal law. There was some dispute over whether the trial would be conducted according to Hawaiian or Whitehall jurisprudence. Luckily for the defendant, the latter prevailed. If he had been found guilty by a Hawaiian judge he would have been hanged by the neck and his nuts eaten by the king.

There went that eating theme again, and he was still feeling stuffed by his late lunch.

As it was, the man was found to be guilty by a British judge, and his punishment consisted of protracted beating about the head and vital organs by an enormous sailor who felt no emotion about the event but in expert fashion used the thick end of a whip, and on occasion his knuckles.

Still, they retrieved only four of the five table knives. They were given to understand, through the agency of gestures by the bruised native, that one of the blades had sunk to the ocean's floor during the swim to shore.

"Ignorant brute," offered Vancouver in the way of opinion, sitting down now on the way back to the ship. "Doesn't have any idea what craft and tradition went into the making of that service, and what an awkwardness the sum of twenty-three is in such affairs."

He was pleased to see that they were rowing

toward the schooner under the muzzles of eight guns Mr. Puget had thought to uncover just in case.

So it was that two hours after the English had hosted the Spanish in a very successful breakfast party, a thin brown man emerged yawning from his hut, walked over sleepily for a piss behind a tree, and went to dig up some white roots he would cut into manageable pieces with his ivory-handled table knife.

It was one of the few pieces, perhaps the only piece, of Indian elephant in his village.

He was sitting in the cozy *pizzeria* across from the hotel. The black guy at a nearby table was singing to himself. He was probably singing that the white guy at the other table was writing in a book.

16

> Wer hat uns also umgedreht, dass wir,
> was wir auch tun, in jener Haltung sind
> von einem, welcher fortgeht?
>
> *Rainer Maria Rilke*

"Now wouldn't you rather be doing this than making war?" asked his new teacher.

This was a totally new kind of teacher. Captain Cook had been like a father to him, and like a son he often saw himself as a continuation of his forebear.

"With you I would rather be doing this, it is true, though you know that if my Admiralty orders me to I must lay siege to your barks," he replied at last.

When he had gone ashore with King Otoo after the short war with the Hawaiians, it had been under a white flag, to retrieve the body of his "father." One day they took a few pieces of it, and the next day they took more pieces of it. They took back most of the body of his "father." When he looked at the naked English leg as it was unwrapped and wrapped again, he thought that it was ugly.

"You know, we were not a great distance from making war, you and I. I should have been unhappy to have put iron through here, or here," said the older man.

He had seen his share and more of dead men, either on his voyages of discovery with Cook, or at arms against the French in the Carribbean actions. A corpse in repose, after the first few, is no great horror; in fact there are times when an aesthete might call it beautiful. As long as it is whole, or reasonably close to that condition.

"I suppose my notion of a happy life would be to spend this kind of time with you, and then to go out and meet the French fact."

"A gallant heart."

"Not gallant so much as ambitious to meet the obligations demanded by the times in which I happen to have lived."

"Well, there is a line of reasoning that would claim you have met the French fact in the past hour."

The younger man laughed with a degree of relief. He had been at sea for twenty-one years, so he was no *naif* in the ways of life aboard naval ships away from port. The hundred men one might find on board a nation's warship may as well, for the long-term isolation from the lights of home, be inmates of one of that nation's prisons.

When he felt the other's lips on his own for the first time, he felt taken as in war, by surprise, so that his brief shame was a kind of patriotism and pride. Soon he moved for his own purpose, as a ship does with the sea, and all at once he thought, I am the younger again, but I have had my days and nights at the helm.

It was not often that he looked upon his own flesh (or any other) wholly naked, not in those days. His condition had been described by the maddening Menzies as bilious colic, and it worried him. He felt betrayed by his own body, and so he was even more skittish when the other bent like an indulgent mother to strip his clothes from him and expose him to himself.

Perhaps that was why he disliked the Scotchman so much, because the Scotchman could read his skin and the colour of his eyeballs as if reading a book of physic. He could look at the outside of his soul's vessel and make an estimation of the events transpiring inside. He could scan the face and read the vitals, augury that no client can forgive.

Yet this other had read his soul through his eyes the day they met at the cove, had read it before it had been fairly perceived by himself. James Cook had showed him how to behave and when to act. This latter master was teaching him to be. A month ago he would have termed the very usage sophism.

"No," he said, taking the other's hand in his and looking at the fingers closely. They were square on the ends, and the nails cut square. They were clean, and free of callous or other asymmetrical marking. "No, I have never been thus brought before in my life."

"By a woman?"

"There has never been a woman in my live save my sisters. I was the youngest child of six, and sailed when I was fourteen."

"Never abed of a wench? Never in the warm islands of the south or the hot ones of the Indies?"

"A few times with whores when I was an able-bodied seaman."

"You are satisfactory now."

"But then chiefly in the way of tradition, my being brought to it by older companions for to initiate me again into another sailor's condition. But I never had any sincere pleasure of it."

"Well, you are not an old man, and you will enjoy for the rest of your career an authority few may emulate. Don't waste your years, my shy Cornish cock."

The years. He coughed not the first time in the bed of his teacher, and he thought of how much he had given for pride and history, and how little they were going to be able to give him back now.

Going back to his own craft in the *Activa's* cutter, he thought about his log and the absence of his greatest discovery in those pages.

17

Commander Vancouver wished he could have been winning Nootka back from the French or the Russians, instead of taking it back by agreement from the Spanish. At least the French and the Russians he had no trouble disliking. Still, had that been the case, Don Juan would at this moment be home in San Blas.

War may make men go round the world, but love makes the world go round. Actually, any novelist, any man of imagination could have told him that commerce was the moving power behind both.

Vancouver knew with his reason that trade was the cause behind all his navy's sailing and fighting, the audience at each smoky skirmish across debris-filled water, that the traders in their beaver hats were the masters of all the boys who perished of yellow fever or grapeshot thousands of miles from their own families. And he hated it. He hated even to acknowledge his own ten shillings a day.

That is probably why, thought Mr. Menzies while he puffed on his pipe at night, the man vents his ample spleen toward the scientific fellows affixed to his command. They were at least allowed to fulfill their entire engagements of a few years without considering that their findings would serve Mammon. Vancouver wished that he could feel the same about the charts he was drawing, rolling, and filing in their waterproof boxes.

That is why he hated this Nootka portion of his commission. He had been conjoined to explore the coast from 30° north to 60° north, and that, after chasing the tricolour, was his chiefest pleasure abroad. Secondly, he was to make the most thorough search ever mounted for the Northwest Passage, and that he essayed with at least half his heart, skeptical as he was from long experience among these inlets.

But he did miss the mouth of the Columbia River, his detractors would say in years to come, and he did miss the Fraser River, which his dear Spanish friends had named Rio Blanco. There was still, even after Vancouver's survey, a standing offer of twenty thousand pounds for the Passage, and a growing number of seagoing persons (though an unchanging quantity of talent) who fancied that they would one day bring a sail eastward into Lake Superior.

It was the third part of his task he did not relish. He was, as it turned out, a fine politician. He had proven that over and over again in his own rise to the position of commander, and in his dealings with the heathen peoples along his track. But like many an excellent statesman or diplomat, he felt most uneasy at the tasks of politics, and wished only to be crashing through some high seas in the unpeopled polar regions.

"If I had wanted to spend my career pursuing the price of animal skins, I would have left the navy and become a lying merchant like that swarthy Mirisch," he said one day as they were plying before a middling wind toward the cove called, as in most artificial amities, Friendly.

"I take it that you refer to John Meares," replied Mr. Mudge.

"It is to clean up the mess he has made with his lying and misdealing that we must rob time from our map making," said Vancouver.

Map making, one would assume on hearing his tone, perfectly combined the vocations of making high art and saving souls.

"And, if I might make so bold, sir," said Z. Mudge, who was never diffident in the memory of any officer of the king's navy, "I might add that it is because of the differences between Mr. Meares and Mr. Martinez that you now find yourself king's commissioner, and consequently promoted to the rank of commander. Sir."

"You have such a sly and flexible tongue, Mr. Mudge. Suppose that while we are about this business at Nootka, we adopt one another's uniforms and tasks. We are about the same size, though I am perhaps a little portlier."

"Not at all, sir."

"A shade stouter, then. You can be George Vancouver for a few days, and I will be Lieutenant Zachary Mudge. By the swiftness of your wit, or its acerbity, I presume you to be a passable dissembler, sir."

Vancouver smiled to show that his line had no dangerous end to it.

"Oh, I am confident that I could masquerade as commander of the *Discovery*, sir. But I fully doubt that George Vancouver could ever pretend to be only First Lieutenant Mudge. Sir."

The trouble with the Spanish had begun when Meares built a house and dock at Nootka, flying the Portuguese flag illegally in order to get around the British East India charter, and trading surplus materials to the Indians for precious furs, especially precious as the Chinese were mad for them, willing to give as much ivory for a seal as would trade for five on the European exchange.

Upon hearing the figures, the Americans came

charging north, led by ships with such apellations as the *Washington*, the *Columbia*, the *Northwest Passage*, the *Yankee Dollar*. Soon there were loudmouth sailors strutting up and down the paths through the villages of Chief Maquinna and Chief Qualicum, buying up every work of folk art in sight, and throwing dollars down the fronts of maidens' blouses.

Three hundred years ago, Balboa had said that the west coast from pole to pole was forevermore Spanish, and the pope agreed with him. San Blas still agreed, and sent Don Estevan Jose Martinez and some elegant escort vessels to Nootka to remove the Americans and Russians and English.

Meares scrabbled up what ducats and hides he could, and sailed for Britain, where a king and parliament, easily impressed by the price of Protestant furs, accepted, if not believing, Meares' account of the ouster, and voted one million pounds to produce a navy that would scare hell out of the Catholics.

All through 1790 there were bluffs and shoutings. Often British sailors and Spanish sailors came to blows in foreign alehouses. Occasionally there were small skirmishes that usually wound up with two Spanish vessels fleeing five British ones. The upshot was that the Spanish were convinced to sign the Nootka Convention, admitting that they had not really built anything north of San Francisco, that their captains were not unduly fond of cold weather, and that the British were to be assured free passage and trading rights north of California. Most specifically, the property seized from John Meares was to be returned to British hands.

This was where the undisguised Commander George Vancouver came in. And he didn't like it, at least at first.

"I did not like the idea at first," he said across the parquet table to Juan Quadra, one evening while they were dining on an enormous fresh salmon.

"All ideas require getting accustomed to, a stretching, shall we say, of the imagination," replied Quadra. He did it through the interpreter because there were other people around. But the particular look in his near eye was in a language at the same time universal and most private.

18

When he came back this all seemed crazy. But hadn't he always thought that that was a good reason for going on? His wife had once said, "I didn't know what to say, so I just kept talking." Everyone stopped and laughed at the time, but now he understood her, and he remembered that she had often been accused by herself and others of making novels out of what other people think is conversation.

What kind of fancy fixed their sailing date for All Fools' Day? He thought of the choice often, and remarked in his journal that they would be commemorated through the years for setting out upon a fool's errand.

All at once he set down his pen and looked at the beginning of the Chinese notebook called "Sailing Boat NB 2220 H." It was all coming together in the way he loved—this had happened other times, and when it did he flew before the wind. He turned to the beginning of the Sailing Boat notebook and saw that he had landed in Trieste and begun writing on All Saints' Day.

A ship of fools then, set upon the purpose of knowledge. The second place they landed was the Cape, and that was familiar to nearly everyone aboard both ships. But the third was far across open sea, forty-five days east of the Cape, at the southwest corner of Australia, the first blank space on the map they would mark. One morning the little *Chatham*, pronounced by Vancouver and its Captain Broughton a poor sailor, led the way as usual to a safe harbour. Now Vancouver, on his own world command, began to name places.

"We have just passed a landfall that will be called from this day, Cape Howe."

"I was going to suggest Cape Why," suggested Mr. Mudge.

The wit of Mr. Mudge was always preferable to the satiric tongue of Dr. Menzies, because the former's humour was not troubled by the balky wind of solemn opinion.

The two ships dropped anchor, and the riggings were brought down while the crews prepared to reconnoitre for fresh water and wild celery.

"What will we title this unprepossessing though mild landing spot?" asked Lieutenant Mudge.

"King George the Third's Sound," replied Vancouver, after the shortest of hesitations.

"I have had occasion to hear that argued more than once," said Mudge, and went to see to the deployment of the guns.

I think we could have set sail upon the thirty-first, thought the commander, or the second. Still, if it was to be a ship of fools, they were *his* fools, hand-picked from earlier voyages to the Pacific coast, or bright careers in the Caribbean campaigns.

Except for the botanist, who was pressed upon him. He was ashore now, gathering plants and making drawings. His patients were in their beds, but a few weeks of good eating would set them right, and they would proceed on Cook's track. With Menzies so eager at his work, they would look like a floating island.

Meanwhile the men gradually reminded themselves of the habitations of their race. They cut from the native bushes a strange wood which they formed into antipodes of British musical instruments. Vancouver smiled, though he had no more than the most ordinary of seamen a love for song. Sometimes a twangle of a thousand instruments seemed to hum around his ears, and he longed for a simple lay.

Still, he felt quite prosperous, half the world before him, and the southern spring just begun, though violent gales from the Pole were a threat that would keep him from venturing too close to the coast of this uncharted continent. But curiously it was not until they were snugged into familiar Dusky Bay at New Zealand, that the greatest, darkest, loudest, most frightening storm Vancouver ever saw smashed into the ships. Salt water coursed over the deck of the *Chatham*, and all hands were convinced, even with anchors out on all sides, that the two ships would be driftwood by morning. But morning saw them still afloat, most wood unbroken, and the Pacific ready for sailing. It might have been a test. It might have been a warning. It was probably just a meteorological fact.

The night before, all torment and trouble, this morning all wonder and amazement inhabited the *Discovery* and the *Chatham*. When they cleared the bay they were smashed by another storm and the two ships separated. A week later the *Discovery* arrived in Tahiti to find that the sixty-foot *Chatham*, that squat, heavy, two-masted, deep-draughted tub of a brig, had preceded its mother ship to port once more.

The sailors liked Tahiti better than anywhere.

Here they got fucked and ate well, and lay around in the sun, getting their red English faces to take on a bit of brown. English faces never do get really brown, kind of a red-brown, with freckles on the forehead. Vancouver said they could do as they chose as long as they obeyed a few rules. For instance, they were to keep to the diet he had set, though they could of course supplement it with such things as mangoes and papayas. And there were to be no male natives on the ship after nightfall.

The women were permitted to live on board, and a lot of people got venereal diseases. Vancouver thought they were fools for it.

But the women *were* really very pretty, and they never stopped smiling, and the men did not often put up great objections to all they heard coming across the black water from a large foreign canoes with folded wings.

Vancouver and Puget were standing by the rail one evening, looking at the moon trying to free itself from some long lateral clouds.

"This is my fifth visit," murmured Vancouver. "I will always love to bide a spell at Tahiti."

"They should call it Ta*her*ti," said Puget.

I'm surrounded by them, thought Vancouver.

19

If the truth be known, and of course we are in a position to know it, or whatever purchase one makes on the truth in a work of imagination, if that is what we are engaged in, that being the entire issue we test here, Vancouver did not really have anything against Dr. Menzies. He was really angry at Banks, not his agent. He hated Menzies, that is true, but it was the hatred for an obvious token, not the anger he reserved for the administrator of the Royal Society. Better a botanist than an agent of the fur trade, for instance.

What was there to hate, really? Certainly not the occasional difference of opinion. Such things should occur between men of sense (though never with other ranks). Certainly not a hatred born out of jealousy. Menzies was a porridge-faced little Scot, with freckles all over his face and the backs of his red hands.

He had a good and thorough naval experience, and was no landlubber aboard ship. On occasion he would be seen in the rigging, climbing like a Barbary ape high over the choppy seas below.

If Vancouver had wanted to make a case against

him he would have called him a devil and shown how science was bent upon the removal of God and His Son from the globe, and that this practitioner of the surgeon's craft had been born in a cold place near the Styx. But the babe had been baptized three years before Vancouver's first sight of this world. And in any case, as to God and His Son, Vancouver had not thought it needful, as most captains did who sail to the ends of the earth from which scarcely half returned to Blighty, to carry a chaplain amongst the crew.

And if the truth be told, after the first six months, there weren't many of the crew unhappy about the lack of a churchman.

When the crew was hired on, Vancouver's set-to with Banks resulted in this compromise: that Archibald Menzies could attend as the Society's botanist, but not as the *Discovery's* surgeon. However, before the party had attained the Cape, Vancouver's surgeon was taken so ill that he must be returned to England. So Vancouver was stuck with the pipe-smoking ginger head as botanist and sawbones.

But at least he came with a seagoing history, having been a surgeon at the Battle of the Saints in 1782, and having served at Halifax Station since. He had also seen the Pacific on an earlier voyage, though with a fur trader, and he never hesitated to offer the good of his experience there. Once at Oahu, when Vancouver could just not get his comfort, the two were standing and looking at several columns of smoke rising from diverse sites on the island.

"They are signal fires," said Vancouver.

"I think not," replied gentle Menzies.

"Signal fires. They are grouping for a prospective assault upon my ships."

"I think they have a much more peaceful intent," said the botanist, and allowed a puff of smoke to arise from his pipe bowl.

"I respect your experience among the Islands,

Mister Menzies, but I am a naval officer of some years' standing, and I say that those conflagrations betide an assault on our position. Now, if you will excuse me, I will make an order for our defence, including yours."

"I too am somewhat of an expert, in my *two* fields, sir," replied Menzies, seeming to enjoy the exchange. "In my field of botany, which perforce includes agriculture . . ."

"Mr. Baker, see to the guns!"

"Which includes agriculture, and which even includes agriculture upon the island before us, I would give the opinion that the local farming folk are engaged in a method of crop rotation and fertilizing known all over the world. We term it the slash-and-burn method; and these people have been observed to employ it upon their sugarcane fields."

Still, it was not till night had fallen and the smoke had been replaced by bright embers in the dark, that Vancouver caused the guns to be unloaded and covered and the gunners sent to their meat and women. By this time the biologist in question was wisely out of sight, choosing seeds to be wrapped and stored aboard the *Chatham* in case of castastrophe for the *Discovery*.

Shortly after they left the Sandwich Islands, they were becalmed for a few days, during which time the officers fretted and the men stayed as much as possible out of sight and out of mind.

But Arch. Menzies was seldom known to sit still or even move about unproductively. He was to be seen establishing himself on the taffrail with a handgun, and presently, having proved himself an excellent shot many years ago outside Edinburgh, brought down the brown albatross that had been following them since they had departed the Islands, in such a manner that it fell upon the open deck of the ship rather than into the drink or among the rigging.

Vancouver watched, and offered respect for the

deed, through only to the universal judges of us all, never to the marksman in question.

The bird, called a gooney by most of the men, measured a little better than seven feet by the span. But not for long. Dr. Menzies soon had it cut into several new shapes, examining it for everything from diet to diseases of the talons. A thoroughly unsuperstitious man, Dr. Menzies, and when he saw what was in the creature's craw, he simply noted it into a commonplace book, with nary a thought for augur.

In case anyone was wondering: yes, this happened on the same day that the English poet was composing his Christian ballad.

In any event, Dr. Menzies seldom read verse, though he did write commendable prose.

Part Two

The Devil Knows How to Row

20

Now he had come back to or to, Vancouver, and complained about the arduousness of the trip. He had risen in the dark in Trieste to catch the Italian plane to Milan. In Milan the first snowfall of the year cancelled flights and he spent a day in the Milan airport before riding on a smoke-filled bus to the other airport and taking a Dutch plane on a bumpy ride over the Alps to Amsterdam. In Amsterdam it was too late at night so the Dutch gave him a room in an American hotel, where he stayed the night, drinking with some Irishmen. The next day was a long day in a Canadian plane, flying over the ocean and the Northwest Passage and through nine time zones, to the city of Vancouver through excellent weather though it was very cold, and there he was.

He was tired. It has been a couple of long days, he said.

"It is my belief," said the first Indian to the third Indian, "that these persons may be gods and they may be men, but that in either case they came to us from the sun."

"That would explain why the canoes you saw were wearing wings," suggested the third Indian.

"The question is, why would anyone, man or god or something in between, come down from the sun to our sea and our land.?"

"To punish us?"

"There you go, speaking out of some habitual framework of guilt. I think you *want* to be punished. I think you enjoy your private sins so much that you desire some confirmation of them, and so you walk around all the time with your shoulders hunched and your eyes looking up guiltily, waiting for Koaxkoaxanuxiwae to poke his beak into the top of your head."

"Okay, not to punish us. Maybe to bring us news of a wonderful new life?"

"What's wrong with the life we live now?" asked the first Indian. "In the summer we go upriver and catch salmon, and in the winter we come to the rivermouth and dig clams. I don't know about you, but I love salmon and clams, and the outdoor life."

"Okay. The world is coming to an end and they are going to take us away on their great winged canoes to their homeland in the sun."

The third Indian's efforts to be creative were noted by his friend with approval. That is why he wasn't impatient with him. A lot of people think that Indians are just naturally patient, but that's not true. Before the white "settlers" arrived there were lots of impatient Indians. It's only in the last two hundred years that Indians have been looking patient whenever there were any white men around.

"Now, come on," he coaxed. "Try to use your imagination. If you were one of these people from the sun, what would you be doing here?"

"I would be looking?" groped the other.

"Go on . . ."

"I would be looking for Indians."

"And what if there were no Indians?"

"Oh, come on, people from the sun would know whether there were any Indians or not."

"Use your imagination. Suppose you were from the sun, and you had come all the way and now you were in our harbour and you didn't see any Indians. What would you be looking for?"

The third Indian thought about it for a while. The first Indian watched him thinking. He saw the third Indian's eyes light up as imagination hit home.

"Clams!" shouted the happy third Indian.

"Exactly. Do you have any idea of how far it is from the sun to our harbour? All that time in the air, surviving on dried fish and the occasional albatross?"

"Clams. And oysters. Prawns."

"After being in the air for all that time. It must take a year to get here from the sun. After being in the air for all that time, can you imagine how nice the first clam is going to taste?"

But the third Indian was lost in thought. He looked as if he were thinking of punishment again. His eyes were looking at the thing that was not there. The first Indian was impatient with him, but he knew his friend's reputation for thinking of the overlooked possibility. It was part and parcel of his guilt, but it was the part to be respected.

"I am thinking about it, and I am imagining that I am one of the people from the sun," said the third Indian sadly.

"I was born to see visions," replied the first Indian. "But I do not see what you are seeing with the sun people's eyes right now. Instruct a poor Indian."

The third Indian shifted uncomfortably, despite all the people who think Indians are always fully comfortable in their natural environment.

"Do you remember when the Kwakiutl came to our previous harbour? Do you remember that they first ate all the fish that we had caught, then they ate a few of us? It was then that we became the fishermen for the Kwakiutl."

"Until the Great Uprising of the People," put in the first Indian.

"Followed by the Great Going Away."

"I am impressed by your suffering of the imagination. You are telling me that these people from the sun will eat all our clams."

"And oysters and shrimp."

"And we will then become the Indians with nothing," said the first Indian, picturing their fate mainly in terms of his wife and children.

"There is an old Haida saying I have heard," said the third Indian, "that says, history will repeat its unhappiest hours upon those who do not remember what happened the first time."

It reminded the first Indian of something. He smiled a small confident smile.

"We will fall back upon the people's secret that sustains us whenever our resources are threatened."

"Precisely."

"One night, as if rising to an undescribed instinct, all our people will quit the victors' sight and vanish into the mist. An unstated number of days later we will have established our dwelling in the holy Strait of Anian, which no invader has ever been able to find. There we will feast upon the most plentiful salmon and shellfish in the world."

"When the danger has passed, we will say a prayer of gratitude to our holy place and return to our workaday world, there to put our minds and bodies to the task of feeding the people at home. A simple life, but one that leaves a lot of time for thinking about things such as gods and men."

"Why don't we stay in the Strait of Anian all the time?"

"Oh, come on. You just have to think for a few seconds and you know the answer to that."

21

Well, in a sense it wasn't just Joseph Banks that Vancouver hated. Archibald Menzies did have an abrasive personality. He was just too . . . sincere. He was *on* all the time, an animated personification of the curiosity of science, aboard this ship. If Vancouver himself had been less a go-getter, he might not have been so riled by the interloper.

That is, he was all the things that Vancouver professed to approve and admire: intelligent, curious, thorough, disciplined, professional. But he was also arrogant. He had the kind of pride that would not allow him to say "Yes, sir," when he was thinking "No, sir."

Before the ships left Tahiti, old Mahow had died, and the natives performed a funeral for their wise old man. In grace and ceremony they had it over a troupe of artists. The rites were largely secret, so the Europeans were not allowed to see any more than what the regular Tahitians saw. Mahow's corpse was carried away to a pretended tomb in the hills, and then he was carried back into the village. From there he was spirited away to the long blue sea, and then he appeared again where ashes of the feast fires lay. This transportation went on for days, while no commerce was allowed among the natives nor with the visitors, no boats were permitted to touch water, no fires could be lit.

All this time, for days and days, whenever Mahow's body came into sight, he looked as if he were still alive, as if his bearers were just lugging him around as they used to, so that he might observe the boatbuilding and the poetry calling. Menzies was tremendously exercised. He was fascinated by the embalming process the Tahitians must hold secret, and he was a good eighteenth-century man; he wanted to add this knowledge to the European store. But the councillors and the bearers would not let him any closer to the mysterious cadaver.

"This is not a specimen, this is our dear old man," they said.

Menzies pulled his pipe out of his straight horizontal mouth.

Vancouver saw him say "Humbug!" or some word of about that shape.

The two of them had a running battle about the size and importance of the greenhouses and relative equipments. The greenhouses had been designed by Sir Jos. Banks, and they were remarkably efficient in all latitudes of the globe. But Vancouver cursed them as piratical invaders.

"Hang it, Menzies, the ship is ninety-nine feet from stem to stern. Thirty-three yards, that is. You, being a scientific man, must realize that it was not constructed to be a plant nursery."

"No, it was not that," agreed Menzies. "But my body was not designed to contain prodigious quantities of pickled cabbage, either. However, I bow to your wisdom in that regard, and only wish that you would let me do my work as I best see fit."

"You have written to your friend at court [meaning Mr. Banks] about your feed, have you not, sir?"

"Only about the payment therefor, sir. That little problem will resolve itself when I collect my pay and expense monies. It is greenhouse space I wish to win now."

"When H.M.S. *Discovery* grows abeam, Mr. Menzies, I will grant you a proportional expansion of space for your weeds."

And as usual, Vancouver stepped off, looking for the need of his attention elsewhere, and feeling foolish therefore. That was the trouble with this short Scotchman: he had a way of making one feel a fool.

And there were already enough fools aboard this ship.

If Menzies had been a poor sailor, Vancouver might have had that over him, and therefore liked him the better. But he was always in the rigging or the boats, handling himself as well as any Jack Dandy.

He was upon the masthead once at 46° 15', and shouted down that he saw water that looked for all the world like the mouth of a river.

"If there were a river there," shouted Vancouver, patronizing the civilian, "I believe that James Cook or George Vancouver, or even Mystic Meares, would have espied it before a rookie from the Royal Society. Press on."

"I thought I saw something like river water, too," said Mr. Bell to Mr. Canby.

"Aye, so did I, lad, but what profits it that we find one more river on the way to the gold, unless that river bring with it water from Ohio?"

Later, talking with the American Gray, who had sailed the treacherous Columbia mouth, Mr. Menzies said of the map-fancier Meares, "Our meeting enables us to detect to the world a fallacy in this author which no excuse can justify."

"We are in need of no liars on this coast," agreed Gray.

"Certainly not among those who would sound a cove and print its fathoms."

Vancouver would have agreed with all this, but he spoke as little as possible with Captain Gray. He had no liking for the Yankee traders in these ambiguous waters. The opportunistic war had been over for only a decade, and it would be a long time till he learned to live with the idea of a country existing for the benefit of its businessmen.

Vancouver had been told by Don Juan Quadra that a man only hates his own defects discovered in another. George tried to see this principle in his view of the busy scientist, and felt that Quadra might have a case. He could just not quite put his finger upon it, that was all.

22

It was just that Menzies was the only gentleman here of his own age. The officers were good; he had pricked out specially. He was special. He knew it when all young. And he was a commander. He had been at sea all his life, and all his life at sea he had been creating the distance between himself and others.

First it was knowing inside himself that he was picked out specially. He was special. He knew it when he was four years old and he had taken to the tide alone on a raft of scrapwood to prove it. He had to be special, or what was the good of being inside his head instead of out there where they all were? In between was the distance, and he kept his distance. He was a good navigator.

It was obvious that Menzies thought himself a good scientist. He gave the signs of his being satisfied to be himself.

So here they were, the only two gentlemen on the ship to have reached their middle thirties. That was not old, but after three-fifths of a life on the salt, after creating all that distance between himself and a Britain full of adequate seamen, that was old, by a scale discovered in one's own abode, that was getting old. He powdered his wig now. That was old.

Since they had left the Sandwich Islands, Menzies had been looking down his throat and listening at his chest. It was a distance closed. In various ways he let Menzies understand that his chest pains and nighttime coughing were not to become subjects of conversation, and the doctor signalled his reply that said yes then, why not? And Vancouver thought why do you not resist me and try to bully me in the way of physicians? Is my condition not of that much moment?

Menzies was thirty-seven and he was himself thirty-five. They should have been sitting to tea together. They were usually civil when thrown together, and politic when they were called upon to speak one of the other. Vancouver did not think to try to imagine what Menzies felt, but himself knew he longed to talk with an equal, had so been longing all his life. But all his life at sea his response to observing an equal had been to rise above that equality.

Now he sailed through the lanes created but unmarked by James Cook, and when in a couple of years he left them in his wake he would have ridden what he loved into the sea he hankered for. He would have become the name they thought of first.

The only way to do it was to sail for the ultimate. He would measure every yard of this crooked coastline. Where the ships could not navigate he would probe with the boats. He would track every inlet to its head, and set his eye to each stop. There would be no faint lines or white cloudy spaces on the charts he took back to Europe's scribes. After learning and seeing the ways of performing better than anyone else, came the chance of touching limits. His boats and his eyes would move to the limits and measure them until there were none remaining unencountered. Then he would go home.

And if he died before he was finished, he would depart having travelled as far as he possibly could. His physician's performance would have been less absolute. Menzies would always be able to ask himself whether there were anything more he could have done.

"I want you to stay out of the boats for now, and to get more bed rest," said the doctor, putting away his implements.

"Give me a draught of something, and get back to your ferns," said the patient.

But he stayed out of the boats while the worst of the attacks weakened him and convinced him that his illusion of youth and physical capability was gone.

Menzies was fond of accuracy, and he enjoyed finding it wherever it showed itself. So he rode happily into each inlet, alighting where he could to sketch polecat or dig up salmonberry. For the surveyors he had a great respect, and he wrote this of the boats and the men he was continuously with:

> It will readily be allowed that such an intricate and laborious examination could not have been accomplishd in so short a time without the cooperating exertions of both Men & Officers whose greatest pleasure seemd to be in performing this duty with alacrity & encountering the dangers & difficulties incidental to such service with a persevering intrepidity & manly steadiness.

In the eighteenth century they were fond of nouns and Latinate abstractions.

Menzies was not, however, taken with the more ceremonial aspects of naval life. While they were ensconced in the harbour of Nootka, they observed the visits of many foreign vessels. Every time a Spanish, Russian, American, even French ship neared the post and fired fourteen or twenty-one guns, the *Discovery* would reply with fourteen or twenty-one of her own, till the air was thick with mixed smoke and mist.

"At last we were become so scarce of ammunition to defend ourselves from the treacherous Indians," wrote Menzies, "that we were obligd to get supplies of Powder from both the Spaniards and Traders before we left the Coast."

He was far more tolerant of the fireworks displays Vancouver put on for the natives, and withheld when the natives misbehaved in the way of thievery and violence. The natives felt about fireworks the way the Admiralty felt about gold and silver.

23

. . . the dreary and inhospitable countries, similar to what has been already noticed in my journal of our excursion during the summer of that year, North Westward from Desolation Sound, would form a package of considerable size, & not so likely to be conveyed with safety by the post thro' this extent of land carriage. I shall therefore refer to the inclosed chart as the best mode of pointing out in what manner our time has been occupied; with only further observing, that in the execution of that irksome, tedious & laborious task, not a moment during the whole summer that could be appropriated to the facilitating the service of our expedition was unprofitably employed.

The track laid down in the Chart, shews the route by which the Vessels proceeded; & the various arms, channels, etc. lying in the different directions from the track, have been finally examined, & their extent determined, by the various excursions of our boats. In one of these cruizes, on the 15th of June last, in the latitude of about 52° 30' & longde 232° our boat crews experienced a malady, which had nearly proved fatal to the whole, & is attributed to some muscles they had eaten, which were of that pernicious quality as very shortly to affect all who had eaten of them with a numbness, first in their extremities, & then over the whole body, attended with dizziness in their head; it would have benumbed the Frenchman who is accustomed to the eating unaccountable fare: this however did not prevent their executing their duty, & the whole of the boats crew pulled their oars, in rowing alongshore, near three hours after they had eaten these muscles; but on the boats landing, about noon, the instant they let off rowing, three of them were seized in such a manner as to be obliged to be carried out of the boat, when John Carter almost instantly expired; the others not feeling this very subtil poison in so violent a degree as the unfortunate man who lost his life by it, drank copiously of warm water, which had the desired effect, in removing the poison; nor did their indisposition continue long after their return on board.

The country we have passed thro' in general this summer, appears incapable of being appropriated to any other use than the abode of the few uncouth inhabitants it at present contains; these however appear by far the more numerous the nearer to the ocean, those inhabiting the interior parts being only in single families or very small parties. As we advanced to the N.W. their appearance, manners, customs, etc., seemed considerably to differ, as did likewise their conduct & disposition, particularly that of the latter after we had passed the 54° of No latitude: those we there fell in with had been much accustomed to the various traders who have lately visited the sea coast, & from them are well supplied with fire-arms & ammunition, by which means they became very formidable to our boat excursions, & in course very unpleasant visitors when assembled in any numbers; as was proved to be the case in two different instances, during our summer's excursion: the one being on the 12th of

August last at Escape Point, near Traitor's Cove, in lat: 55° 37' & Longde 228° 30' where myself, accompanied by Mr. Puget, in the pinnance, on a very long excursion, nearly had, & I believe inevitably would have, been cut off, and everyone murdered, but for the timely assistance of the Launch, by which means we escaped without the loss of any lives on our side, & only two of our people badly wounded, who have since perfectly recovered. The other instance was not far remote from the same station, where Mr. Johnstone, in returning to the ships from a similar excursion, was, on the 3rd of September, near Cape Caamano, suddenly surprised by the sallying out of near two hundred & fifty Indians in their canoes, all armed, and at once starting from a behind a point of land, approacht hastily towards the boats, with every appearance of hostile intentions, but on some musquets, & a swivel loaded with grape-shot, being fired near them they desisted, & the boats passed by unmolested.

The produce & aspect of the country we have thus explored differs in no material degree from what has been already described North-Westward from Desolation Sound; excepting the sea-otter being every where in the greatest abundance, though like the inhabitants of the country are more numerous the nearer to the ocean: & nearly the whole of the natives, which in our different excursions we have fallen in with, are well verst in commercial pursuits, & seldom visited us without bring sea-otter skins, which they generally disposed of, though at an exorbitant price, of which during the season I believe near three hundred were purchased by the different persons on board; & had such been our pursuit there is little doubt, but we might have collected any quantity we wisht to take.

I have thus in a cursory manner mentioned these circumstances of advantage & disadvantage, that it may serve for the information of future visitors, the extent of this mode of . . .

24

He was amused to consider that he had flown over the Rockies and the Alps in one day. In elementary school he'd learned the world: there are seven continents, five oceans, and four great mountain ranges: the Rockies, the Andes, the Alps, and the Himalayas.

A rift in the clouds had shown the coastline near Newcastle. England rose out of the sea, but its surface is really flat.

In the antipodes they had sailed into fjords that will shrink your scrotum, but he could still never get used to the mountains that rear suddenly out of the mist and up from the water, so that the land you have been making for is not in your fancy or before you, but beside you, and above your mast. A sailor from Britain must always know that experience as the resolute image of the foreign. Coming from a civilized arrangement of chalk cliffs to mark an edge, and the flat greenery with reasonable fences, and trees grouped around church or house, a greenery that stretched inward from that white edge, a Briton comes to mountains miles high as if to islands on the moon. Might as easily conceive the sails as wings, and fly to a meeting on the moon.

These men aboard these two ships, or other British two hundred years earlier in the same waters, their normal state is landless, deep sea men surrounded by what is never human like a ship. Yet they were all born in some building set on land. Their normal place is the deep sea, but their natural home is upon the unwavering earth. The time it took Britain to crack free of the lowlands is equal to the time it will take her men to pull free of their cribs in Epsom and Stoke.

So imagine their mixture of sentiments as they sail now, deep sea sailors with land on both sides of them, and the land covered foot by foot with fir trees, and above them the great blue rocks that stand in the sky as if pulled that way, upward.

A person was busy working. This was a job, not a passage to Cologne or a summer's weekend. But there were moments when quick rocky death did not threaten, and one by another watched, as did this captain, and thought: this is nothing like the places where men and women live.

Yet it looked, when they walked ashore, as if it were a garden prepared for human habitation. Wild roses bloomed in the bushes. Gooseberries and blueberries, huckleberries and currants, waited to be plucked. A party of men would round a bend and discover twenty ducks sitting upon the lagoon, resting on their own way north. Long shapes of flesh lay in the last few hundred yards in each narrow river. Long sandy beaches were strewn with shiny grey driftwood. It was quiet and new, but the rocks were old, as if one were looking now at the state of the world soon after its preparation.

People arriving at this place just had to go off into it, to see it all. Yet there was so much of it.

And the first carved pole they found seemed not an intrusion in a paradise. Rather it was as if the pole had been abandoned, as if it had not been enough for a person to cling to in an attempt to survive in this deep green element. It made the place seem old, all right, but not the old of a Norman church in Sussex or a village in Palestine. Here a piece of human fashioning left a few decades ago, is old.

"Why are they not lonely, Mr. Menzies?"

"They are, commander."

"Are they, then?"

"From our point of view."

The two did not often have such quiet conversations, and usually one just had to imagine them.

"It must be strange to live among such an extreme landscape," suggested Vancouver.

"Yet as we know, there are men who live upon the desert and in the snow," said the surgeon.

"And in Scotland," added the captain.

"It is we who come here and fancy it odd to live among mountains and so far from Mayfair. You fear it, then?"

"I have come to work here."

"You imagine living here, and you fear the idea, then."

"A peculiar verb of your choosing, Mr. Menzies." Vancouver turned away from him.

"It is because you take a mountain for a god and a god for a father," Menzies went on. "The people who live here have conversed with me long upon this theme, and at my urging. They deem the mountains to be mountains, that and whatever advantage they can make of that. They are true Western man."

"It is not my desire that I take high land to be a deity," said Vancouver after a while. "For then, what makes that of the sea?"

"Why, one runs away to sea. That is what one does with the sea," said Menzies smartly.

25

At Port Townsend the three boats had entered protected water that caused the officers to believe that here indeed was the gold they had been halfheartedly looking for. It would have been impossible to conjure a geography more like Eden. Douglas Firs reached high and scattered the sunlight on the forest floor carpeted with brown needles. Beyond them rested two snow-covered peaks, which Vancouver had named Baker and Rainier, for his lieutenant and for a rear-admiral influential enough to advise upon promotions.

The moss that covered the rock near the bay was speckled with tiny round flowers. Menzies was taken by some delicate purple bell-shaped blossoms that appeared always on solitary stalks wherever they walked. Clover bloomed and attracted the bees that left savoury honey in the red cedars. Large nests constructed of twigs topped many of the highest firs, and eagles' wings could be seen from time to time, spread silently at heights no arrow had ever reached.

On the shoulder where the bay met the Chimacum River, they found the settled and peaceful remains of an Indian village. These consisted of a midden of mussel shells, rocks for drying trout fish, three piles of ashes, a smokehouse, drainage trenches, several stakes driven into the easy soil, with heads on them. These were brown and quite dry, but some of the eyes were still there. There were also quantities of burnt bone around and in the ashes.

"Are these the sport of your friendly fisherfolk and tribesmen?" asked Mr. Vancouver of Mr. Menzies.

"I disbelieve it, my captain," replied that worthy. "I take these relics for the friendly folk themselves. I believe further that it would benefit us to determine the identities of those who disjoined and fired them."

"In the meantime we will establish camp upon the other side of this stream, and we will set a double contingent of pickets this evening and for all the evenings to come save those we are fortunate enough to spend on board our ships."

"We could spend this night there quite easily," said Menzies.

"I am surprised at you, sir," said Vancouver, who was sitting down with care for his aching body. "The New World is your greatest laboratory and your matchless joy. We will spend this night on no rocking waves, but where the newmade Adam himself might lie him down."

Menzies was happy enough with this decision, though not with the language of its description.

"If you hap to lose a rib during your sleep, sir, we will find no great shortage of them on the earth across the river."

"If I find upon the morn an Eve as pretty as the lady who brought us this far, I shall mourn the loss of no rib," said the captain.

"What would thou with an Eve?" asked Menzies *sotto voce* but loud enough that the other might chance to hear him and choose to pretend he had not. Menzies hoped this was the case.

"You see that red tree?" asked Menzies. "It belongs in the Orient, just as its white cousin to the south belongs in Van Diemen's Land."

"They are trees, Bones, and they can be cut down and shaped into planks to keep our souls afloat. That they are here is evident to the eye. It needs not wonderment."

This was Mr. Broughton, who spent most of his spare time in sleeping.

"To you they are trees, perhaps. To a man of science they are signs, messengers, almost as omens and portents. They tell me that there had been as long ago as that tree's life a passage to and from Asia, and that is a very old tree. Who made that passage, sir?"

"A bird with an upset stomach."

"You have sailed from New Zealand to Port Townsend. Did you encounter any birds travelling west to east other than those that hung in the air over our mast?"

"Here come your Indian friends. Mayhap they flew here from India while no civilized ship was about to see them."

"I for one have not ruled out the possibility," said the scientist, waving to the approaching natives.

"Or mayhap they came here from the sun on the back of a giant bird," said Broughton, and wandered off. He didn't like to be around the Indians. He said they smelled as if they slept with their fish.

But he did not fail to break his boring diet every time these fishermen brought around their fare: salmon, sole, clams, oolichans, smelt. Vancouver could have designated a crew of his own men to catch seafood, but guessed it to be more efficient and more politic to trade a bit of steel for the natives' catch, knowing their pride that caused them to bring their best luck to the Europeans.

While the metal was being bartered for the seagoing flesh, in the complex manner of these people in their dealings with the whitish foreigners, Menzies approached the subject of human bones and heads, in a roundabout manner that reached this far after a half hour:

"During the general run of things, in times of great hunger, or in the course of particular ceremonies, do your people ever eat a little bit of human bodies? I'm not accusing you now, you understand. It is my vocation to collect knowledge for my people, and this I do without blaming anyone for anything."

"I have never eaten a person," said the first Indian.

"I also am innocent of eating any person," said the second Indian.

They contrived by way of gestures that were supposed to be thought unconscious, to indicate the seasoned flounder they had delivered.

"Is there any tradition in your culture of eating people? Slaves or elders or captives, anything of that sort?"

The two Red Men looked at one another and then toward the forest where they would go if things worked out.

"It seems as if I did hear something once about our forefathers eating people long ago before the time of the Great Flood," offered the first Indian.

"Earlier this summer we found a village that had been abandoned within the month. It was attended by heads on sticks, and human bones thrown into the fire," said Menzies, examining the cheeks of a sockeye.

"There is a rumour, unsubstantiated, that a remnant of that ancient people-eating society survives. They are entirely isolated, of course," said the second Indian. "Nobody I know has ever come across them."

"You were fortunate perhaps to find one of their camps," said the first Indian. "It is said that they move around often."

"Indeed, we were fortunate," Menzies agreed. He signalled to a sailor to take the fish to stores.

"We will see you again soon," suggested the first Indian, betraying a little of that impatience the Red Man had before the coming of the Europeans.

"Uh, one more question, I pray you," said Menzies, walking with them.

"We will do our best to supply an answer," said the first Indian.

"Thank you," said Menzies. "My question is, and I know that you can only tell me what you have heard, and I know that knowledge is sketchy in this area because the activity is so rare. But I would like to know for what purpose these elusive people-eaters eat people."

They had reached the edge of the trees. Now they stopped, the signal that this was as far as the two Indians would be accompanied. The second Indian just plainly looked away into the forest, while the first Indian tested one of the steel blades against the bark of a fir trunk. He spoke at last, but not much.

"I cannot be dead certain, but I believe I remember hearing that one person would eat a second person in order to consume that second person's imagination."

"Consume it?"

"To transfer it from the person being eaten to the person eating."

"Imagination?"

"To take it over, in the belly."

"To eat a person?"

But they were gone, somewhere before him behind the salmonberries. It was all he would hear today. They were gone from his sight, and so why think about them more?

26

Of a sudden he was there with her in the long house. She gave him a hot brown stare. His boots were crusted with the mud of yesterday's beach. So were his plain brown breeches. His shirt was soiled, his waistcoat grabbed on askew. There was a wide rip in the front skirt of his coat, and all looked slept in. She thought he was as exciting as any man she had ever seen. Other women had told him that a glance from his eyes had turned their blood to Drambuie. His swollen roger was perceivable behind the stuff of his breeches.

He gestured with a draughting pencil and she followed him out of the building. He was always happy to escape that odour and get out under the cedars again. She caught up to him and walked two paces behind him to their place in the woods.

There he put his instruments away and settled himself against the mossy rock upon which he had remarked *bryophytics* highly imitative of those green-grey carpets found on the ancient building stones of his old university. The university on the hill, they had called it, and what amorous adventures he had experienced there would fill a book, but not a real life.

She stared at him again, from up close this time, and offered one of the words he had taught her.

"Suck?"

"Darling, I am not about to refuse, but one does wish for a moiety of circumspection, a little more of the hare-and-hounds."

As she was pulling at his breeches, he noticed, a few paces away, the first bloom of some *clintonia* he had not seen here before.

She had his roger out now, and he had a second to enjoy the cool Pacific air upon it. That was always a pleasure, and really, something a person could manage any time one wished, but one seldom did.

Now she held it before her eyes, between the fingertips of both hands, and stared at it solemnly. It was as if she were about to plunge it ceremoniously into her heart. A bead glistened at the tip like nacre.

Then out came her pointed tongue and she ran her pointed tongue up her side of it, along the great vein, from cool scrotum to hot ruby. Then she went down again, turning her head sideways so that the tip of her tongue could continue, and it did, briefly into his little hole. Quietly he spread his knees wider one from the other.

She looked up, her black hair falling in front of both shoulders, and she said two more of the new words he had given her.

"Fuck now?"

"More suck," he said, placing his left hand and his right hand on the top of her head. How quickly we can all be turned to savages, he thought. While she placed the round smooth glans gently between her lips, an image of brown heads on stakes entered his mind's eye.

One of her hands held the shaft like a flute, the other was under him with a finger a little into his aperture, and her head was bobbing up and down. Her heavy hair lay against his white belly and hip. She was quite loud, sucking and breathing, and he was reminded of something. It came to him: she sounded like a dolphin surfacing to blow air, and then like a dolphin she sounded.

He thought he would froth, but then she stopped, and stood up beside their gooseberry bush. His flesh towered, red and waving back and forth in front of him, as he watched her taking off her simple clothes. In the filtered sunlight her skin was marvelous, unlike his porridgy covering. Her black hair hung down, greasy and heavy, breaking over her high budding breasts.

She spoke again, and this time it was not a question.

Before going to sea, to the southern islands and the American coast, he had never done it outdoors. He had not even dreamed of doing it outdoors. Even now there were things he didn't like about it, the fir needles in his knees, the insects, the chill that sometimes followed. But there were advantages that outweighed those discomforts. There were no embarrassing noises to he heard in the next apartment, such as creaking bedsprings, or a bed that raps against the wall of milady's chamber. The members of the family did not have to be passed on the way out or in.

But most important of all was the exhilarating sense of exposure. Not only the nakedness of one's body to the clime, but the possible proximity of bears or snakes, or native hunters.

She smelled quite a lot like a dolphin, too. He didn't love it, but he didn't hate it, either.

Her body was nice and big on him, her brown thighs full and pleasant to his touch, as she worked for fun, as she slopped up and down on his roger, and all of a sudden he threw up his hips and came into her. She felt it and came almost immediately afterward, but still she moved, reaching for more.

When he opened his eyes he espied two shy *gen-*

tianella on the far side of the pile made of their clothes. When he closed his eyes he felt the lovely urge of her body mining its lust, he heard the air rushing from her chest with every bump, the sloshing extrusions of air from below, and he formed a picture in his mind's eye of Mrs. Banks.

27

He heard a jet liner taking off, the roar at this distance generalized and coming in rolling waves, and he remembered that during the night he had dreamed of unexpectedly flying to a strange Central American city with his wife; so he was led to picture the inside of the fuselage, noticing that in that tube few people knew each other while together travelling like a bullet to Tokyo or Montreal or a quick death.

But what he noticed principally while looking at this picture was that if the airplane is flying to another city on the continent, nearly all the passengers are men, and if it is flying across the ocean to another continent, half the passengers are women and children.

There was a time when things were quite the other way round.

The first trouble with the Indians came while Peter Puget was surveying the complicated sound that would be named after him. One morning as they filled the boats and prepared to go ashore for firewood, they espied thirty quiet Indians along the edge of the land, bows in the hands they carried by their sides.

"Stow some worthless trash to trade to those monkeys for their goodwill," said the perfectly-dressed Lieutenant Puget.

"Aye aye, sir."

If you hang around a naval vessel for any length of time you will often hear someone saying aye aye, sir. Peter Puget loved to hear sailors and even the ship's master say it.

Now he wantd to hear the Indians say it, or something equivalent. He gestured for his megaphone, and when he had it, raised it to his handsome face and shouted shoreward.

"You mouse-eating savages are in luck today! We are bringing ashore some worthless trash to brighten up your lives!"

Then he told his chief to make ready the boats. When he did that the thirty Indians fitted their very long bows with very long arrows, and pointed them at the mariners.

"Mr. Bradshaw," said Puget, striking a pose he had seen in large paintings of great admirals, "will you offer our friends a sniff of the vintage?"

That was the way he liked to order a salvo of grapeshot. The gunner fired two guns into the sea between the red men and the white. The resulting disruption of the water was sufficient to induce peace. The Indians let the strings of their bows back gently, and accepted the worthless trash from the landing party that included a contingent of marines with muskets.

All but one of them did, that is. A young bowman who had been standing to one side and up to his knees in the sea, had been struck in the eyes with grape. His arrow plunged into the sea twenty yards in front of him, and his bow fell from his hands into the water, from where it would be retrieved an hour later as a souvenir. The blinded and gravely injured youth turned and stumbled from the water and up from the beach, striving blindly to escape the scene of his pain.

It could then have been seen that the grapeshot had struck him full with its horrible force. He was bleeding from several lacerations, and his nose and mouth had been torn apart as well as his eyes. With his gory hands held to his tattered face he stumbled a hundred feet into the bushes and fell face forward into a small depression.

One of the marines followed him. The other tribesmen were deterred from following by sincere marines with levelled muskets.

Peter Puget never learned Vancouver's trick of assuming the natives' tongue; and he was much more tolerant than was Vancouver in the matter of sailors' treatment of dark-skinned people. Puget was a career officer all right, but he was no innovator, no inventor; however the navy did things was fine with him, in fact more than fine: it was fitting.

So he assumed that the missing brave was being justifiably roughed up a little by the missing marine. But after a space of fifteen minutes he began to worry that something unforeseen might have happened to bring about a disadvantage to his man. For this reason he sent two others in search of him. Unfortunately for the first marine, both of these latter two were serious Wesleyans.

Vancouver had that man put in irons for the rest of the voyage, until he could be delivered to civil authorities in England. But first he had him flogged.

What had he done to deserve the commander's wrath? He had gravely injured the good relations so carefully wrought between the map makers and the inhabitants. He had broken the clear discipline that was understood to be an essential part of Vancouver's every voyage. And he had transgressed the laws of both civilized human society and the Almighty.

When the two Methodists had found him he

had gone entirely to hellish bestiality. He had pulled the animal skins from the bleeding young aborigine, dropped away his own breeches, and was treating the Red Man the way a depraved farm boy treats a fat ewe. Worse was his derangement, as neither he nor the witnesses could swear to whether he was violating a wounded and dying Indian, or a corpse.

Puget, on hearing the facts he did not welcome, could do little else. He thanked the two men for arresting the beast, and gave him over to Captain Vancouver's displeasure.

Vancouver sentenced him to two hundred lashes, to be administered over eight occasions, the ship's company to witness on each occasion.

Upon that first occasion Vancouver summoned the surgeon to stand with him. It would of course be Menzies' occupation to attend the man in case an errant lash were to strike his eye, or some similar mishap.

"What this man, if that indeed is what we are to call him, what this man, I say, has done, is worse than the acts perpetrated upon Captain Cook's body by the Islanders. They, at any rate, had not th'advantage of Christian government," said Vancouver.

They watched the perspiring boatswain's mate lift the whip and throw his whole body and arm into another stroke. The leather snapped loudly against itself and thudded into the mariner's trunk. Vancouver grimaced. Menzies did not. He knew the secrets closed up inside the human body and the skull. He had seen flesh treated to the widest possible range of punishments and investigations.

Vancouver flinched ever so slightly again. His eyes closed and his lips opened a crack. On the next stroke the tip of his tongue was visible for a half second at the corner of his mouth. Yet, thought Menzies, he has done this several times on this trip, and the offence *was* odious.

"At the least," said Menzies, "when he was discovered at his heinous work, he was not heard calling a woman's name."

"What do you intend by that remark, mister?"

He was angry and suspicious, but his best sense told him to remain calm for now. The whipping continued.

28

They followed the shoreline because what else was there? Especially with the clouds and rain and sometimes fog, and all the time the riptide and all the islands, what else was there? They followed the shoreline of the continent, if that was what it was, and the shoreline was seldom a question of north and south; it went through every degree on the compass. How it got eventually and generally north was difficult to see, or often so.

But their flag sailed each foot of the way, and it took Vancouver and his officers little time to understand that their task would consume several summers, that the men in the boats would pull their oars more than a million times, that the lover of facts would have a belly full of them for years to come.

Plus this fact: the Indians were not all the same Indians. Some of them killed others. All of them had been on the coast since God had here dropped them, of certainty longer than the history of European visitation. The land was a savage beauty, and of a scale that can kill you. You can die if you are unlucky, you can die if you do not at all times watch carefully, and you can die if the work and the weather are too demanding, if you are not enough or they are too much.

Contrast the victorious and brave stories of those who were here earlier and luckier. Juan de Fuca himself entered at Cape Flattery and reached the Atlantic in twenty days, he said. Then instead of sailing directly for Europe, he turned back to the Pacific, to double check. He had, said he, an obligation of honour in the matter of men and trade goods left on the Pacific side.

The Portuguese sailors who have been fishing the Grand Banks for most of Christian history, sailed the Northwest Passage to China and back again in the 1540's.

A hundred years later, according to the Spanish claims, Admiral de Fonté sailed from ocean to ocean upon the Rio los Reyes, and thus set the scene for Catholic propriety in the territory. But try as they might, English historians could find no irrefutable evidence that the Admiral ever existed. That did not deter English seamen (and officers) from believing de Fonté a historical fact.

In 1728 the Bering Strait became a historical and geographical fact. It was not the Strait of Anian. It was to be the dramatic intercalation between two continents. But the ground on the one side belonged to the same plan as did the ground on the other side, especially in the winter. Vitus Bering was not paid well enough for remaining on that cold and distant water.

Nevertheless, a quarter century later, Delisle's maps showing the Strait of Anian formed the basis for the charts in every palace along the Rhine and the Danube, and in the Palazzo Vecchio in Florence. In 1788 John Meares reported that he had followed these maps to the Passage, and in 1790 Alexander Dalrymple caused the Delisle charts to be carried on British ships and traded to friendly admiralties in exchange for their informations. They included the mysterious and even frightening feature that Juan de Fuca placed at the gate to Anian, a colossal stone pillar of totally unknown origin. It was a landmark seen by earlier luckier mortals but never by Cook or the Spaniards, or Vancouver.

Meares said that in 1789 the American Captain Gray, in the *Lady Washington*, sailed past the pillar and into the Strait of Anian. Meares' book published a chart of that legendary voyage. (But two years later Mr. Menzies with Lieutenant Puget, falling into conversation with Captain Gray, brought up the facts of Meares' book and the fortunate passage, whereupon the Yankee disavowed both. Fancy, we are permitted to see once more, does not hesitate to make its face plain where there is money to be claimed.)

But James Cook had been an efficient navigator, a purposeful manager, and a pessimist in matters of mysterious sea creatures or uncharted islands. Cook's River was his first deviation, and came upon his British fame. So when George Vancouver was expressly enjoined to prove all the claims made by his predecessors, he came to the task with his absolute eye and heart.

In Meares' book, so popular with Mayfair and Whitechapel, there is a plate that sets young lads to dreaming. It displays the Strait of Juan de Fuca, seen from near Tatoosh Island, and shows the great stone pillar. A lot of sailors must have missed it in the fog.

At moments when he was entirely alone, and resentful, and aching through his chest, he wished two wishes. He wished for the Strait of Anian, and he wished that his command would put to rest forever any hope for a quick waterway to the North Atlantic.

He was glad to be a year away from the "closet philosophers" who sat upon cushioned chairs with high cushioned backs to complete Cook's charts, though during the great height of his career James Cook deflated their most greedy theories. They had replied that he was "hasty."

When he knew for certain that his thoughts were entirely alone, he thought at last of Cook's River and the old captain who fell at the last "amongst the pursuers of peltry."

When he had collected as much as he could of his father's body and caused it to be retired with proper respect and a requisite expenditure of gunpowder, he had fought down an urging to touch his tongue to the insulted flesh, to taste his continuance. For the next week he had vomited all his meals into the ocean.

Now he would assemble a continent, and let the powder puffs choke on it.

"The sea," said Menzies to him in mid ocean, "is also a garden."

29

Puget Sound, after many twists and false hopes, came to an end, so that was not it.

There would be others; but they were so far north now, there must be one soon if there was to be one. Next there was the waterway to be named, no matter what it turned out to be, after Burrard. It was a deep one and wide, but it too came to an end. But the shores here were so pleasant, and the Capilano Indians so gentle, that it was no disappointment, Burrard Inlet. They stopped over for a while.

Menzies went up the lower slopes of the snow-topped mountain, and Vancouver went to see the government of the Indians. They were friendly and curious about everything. One day a crew of sailors laid out their seine net, and when it was time to draw it in, Vancouver alerted the Capilanos, who crowded around to watch from their canoes. They shouted and gestured, and then as the net was pulled free of the water, they remained utterly silent because it was plain empty.

To them it must have been a frightening moment

from a religious point of view. But the white men just seemed to be going about their business.

"Aw fuck it," one of the white men said.

"Bully beef tonight, lads."

"Ah, shit!"

The first Indian's eyes opened wide. He crinkled his forehead and said his first ceremonial English words.

"Aeh, shitt!" he said.

The second Indian, understanding that the imprecation was an essential part of a ceremony having to do with assuring the Great Spirit that one was thankful for His care despite a disappointment this time, shouted louder than anyone thus far.

"Aeh, Shitt!"

"Yeah, ah, shit!" yelled an English sailor.

All the Capilanos, about fifty of them, stood up in their dugout canoes as only they could do and shouted in unison, so that their deep Indian voices resounded from a curved rock-face a mile away:

"Aeh, shitt!"

Hanging by the belly over a rail, sitting on a tackle box with face in hands, lying on stomach and with fists pounding the deck, the sailors laughed and laughed. The Indians sat back down in their canoes and laughed.

Vancouver stood on the bridge and smiled. He never used that kind of language himself, but here at the edge of the world, what timber and rocks would know a curse from a wedding song? Arch. Menzies sat at a deal table, making paragraphs in his notebook.

Early that evening the Capilanos brought five dozen river-mouth salmon to the *Discovery*, and that night there was a big cookout on the long sandy beach under the protection of the north shore mountains. The Englishmen ate the Indian salmon, and the Capilanos drank the English rum, and everyone got happy and sleepy, and it was one of the best ever Friday nights enjoyed there. No one got mad, no one got hurt, and everyone except Vancouver and some of his officers slept in on Saturday. Menzies was seen to come aboard very late that morning, with flowers in his hair.

"Just doing my job, Your Majesty," he said to Vancouver, as he took his gear to the greenhouse. He often referred to his captain as George the First, but seldom to his face, and then only circumspectly.

"How is your chest cold?" asked Vancouver. "I hope that you have not been allowing duty to lead to a neglect of your body. Certainly lying upon damp ground all night is not going, in the end, to promote the interests of science."

"What I was doing last night was less in the aegis of science, and more aptly designated an art," said the botanist, lighting his pipe.

"Phew! Where did you get that foulsome tobacco?" asked Vancouver.

"Oh, I ran out of tobacco long ago. This is something the Indians showed me. It does smell strong, doesn't it?"

It is said with justice that the Capilanos were the great imitators of the Coast, and most critics with tolerance will agree to the ambiguity of that statement.

So it was hard to say anything in a hortatory way, without hearing an echo from forest or surface.

"Avast!" someone would shout from the shrouds.

"Avast!" would come the unexpected reply from the stand of mountain ash trees on shore.

So there were always Indians around, asking permission to try their hands at the European oars, belaying pins, sextants, and coffee cups. It got to be a nuisance at times, but it was a lot better than shooting and getting shot at.

Late one morning Able Seaman George Delsing was surprised to see four canoes out in the middle of the inlet, setting out a seine; it looked as if it were made of hemp. He made certain that he was there to watch when the boatmen hauled it in. It was pretty heavy with hopping fish and a couple of dolphins. The Indians were always doing that to white men. Maybe their success was due to their great patience.

The last day around Burrard Inlet, Peter Puget heard a noise, and looking up from his chart, saw a group of about a dozen Capilanos walking toward his camp. They were elbowing one another, laughing, pushing one another to the front of the knot of gesticulating black-haired men. They came to a dancing, stamping, giggling kind of a halt. One punched another in the ribs. A third chewed on the end of his hair.

"What can I do for you noble savages?" asked Puget. He had not learned anything from his experience at Port Townsend.

One of them said something loudly in Indian, and one held his arms in front of him and said, "Poo, poo!"

"Poo, poo?" enquired Puget.

"Something about our muskets," said Menzies, who was making a sketch of the group.

"All right, give them one boom boom," said Puget.

A marine primed his weapon and fired, knocking a crow off the top of a cedar snag. His friends applauded, and one went to retrieve the carcass.

The visitors were excited. They laughed and pointed and stepped on each other's toes. At last it became clear to the Englishmen that they wanted to try the musket themselves. Puget agreed that they could fire it once. He instructed the marine to ready the weapon again and give it to someone. This done, the marine held it out toward the Indians.

They jostled and leaned backward and stepped up and down, and finally the first Indian felt himself pushed out in front of his fellows. Either that, or they had all taken a step backward without warning him.

He took the heavy thing the man handed over to him. Recalling as much as he could about the way the white man had handled it, he got it to his shoulder. For a full minute he held his finger to the trigger, trying to summon the nerve to squeeze it.

At last it went off by itself, with a horrible loud and close noise. The recoil knocked him back, but he was still standing, and he was still holding the musket. His companions clapped their hands and whistled.

He had shot the table that Puget's chart was on, and the chart along with most of the table was blown into shreds.

"Ah, shit," said James Green, a carpenter's mate from Leeds.

"*Aeh, shitt!*" hollered the Indians.

30

A day after the Indian shot Puget's map table to kindling, the two ships were sailing through a bit of a storm into another waterway a few miles north. This one Vancouver named after Admiral Earl Howe. Never had he felt so excited about the prospects for the Passage, and wanted it to bear the name of Britain's commander-in-chief for America. He was basically skeptical, of course, but there was a feeling that crept over him that he could not explain, that he had not felt before with such intensity. It was as if a spirit's hand were laid upon his shoulder, and as if he were looking back on a successful passage to Hudson's Bay rather than ahead to an open field of possibilities.

It was a cold grey morning, with dark clouds dragged up the sky before them, and a hard wind pushing across their path. It was as if they had passed from midsummer into early winter. They had left a month of quiet afternoons on gentle slopes or even meadows, with natives friendly or difficult, but in any case present on a generous earth, and now they entered, under rolling black clouds, a passage enclosed upon both sides by mountains that plunged almost straight into the deep sea, with snow on their tops, and not a sign of human habitation or its possibility.

It was as if they were entering a path refrigerated by its origin in Henry Hudson's bleak seas. Long thin braids of water fell a thousand feet over the rock faces into the grey chuck and produced the only sound other than the creaking of the planks. The passage stayed as wide as it had been at its mouth.

Vancouver was so thrilled that he did not allow himself to say anything other than his commands. He scarcely permitted himself to think. If this was his best hope it was also his last one. After that the hand on the shoulder would be without doubt or hope a fantasy.

He did not once think of the twenty thousand pounds. He stood out in the open, watching for any sign of narrowing water or a shorter chain. The rain whipped at him from the side from time to time.

Menzies was attempting to keep his pipe lit. *He* allowed himself to think. This is what he thought: Here we go, yet another once-in-a-lifetime experience.

Imperceptibly, the rainfall became light and then ceased altogether. The gusting wind evened out into a subtle and companionable breeze. The surface of the water turned from grey to a deep green, and the *Discovery* no longer bashed its way through waves that had been coming from two directions at once. Now the sloop seemed to ride on top of the water rather than through it. The sails bellied forward like the torsos of harmless women seen in paintings by Peter Paul Rubens. The boards no longer complained, and their noise was replaced by a faraway musical sound, something that resembled choral singing, as if a choir in a church across the square were performing Handel's Coronation Anthem, Number One.

As they sailed farther into Howe's River the ships picked up speed, *Discovery* seemed to be skimming on the tops of the small waves now, and the sails billowed evenly. Vancouver looked in front of him to where the *Chatham* always was, and he saw her lift free.

Then he felt the bow of the *Discovery* go up, and the surge of power as the sails caught and the waters dropped below and behind them. He braced himself while the craft bumped through the rocky air above the first peaks of the Coast Range. He saw the *Chatham* break through the cloud cover, and a few seconds later they were enveloped in grey cloud that turned white, and then they were through. The sun shone white over the miles and miles of cumulus, and picked out the moisture shining on the sails of the two ships alone in all that fluffy sea, coursing eastward effortlessly now, at home in the jet stream.

When they crossed the last of the Rockies and began the long straight cruise over the prairies, the clouds broke up and swiftly disappeared, and the great green table lay for hours beneath their hulls. They did not see another ship during the whole passage across. The sun was brilliant on their canvas, and below them their shadows crossed more than one lonely-looking native village.

"Those superstitious heathens would be fouling their breeches, if they had the decency to be wearing any," remarked Peter Puget.

"In any case, they will be conjecturing upon the question of whence we have come," mumbled the surgeon.

There was an unexpected calm aboard the ships now that the Passage was fairly underway. The elation the commander had felt before entering Howe's River was now settled into a long comfortable pleasure.

They came upon clouds again as the prairies were about to give way to the Pre-Cambrian Shield. Vancouver felt the change in the sails as the ship slowed at once and began its long descent to Hudson's Bay. First the *Chatham* and then *Discovery* nosed bumpily into the clouds, finding below them a nice early summer day, overcast but dry. The water on the Bay was only slightly rippled, and their landing was long and smooth.

"A nice flight," said Mr. Baker, who was relieved to be back on the surface, though it was the East now, and so it was going to be humid, and he would commence the snuffling and wheezing that so much annoyed his commander. That was because the sounds reminded him of the mortality inside his own chest, he told himself.

"Yes, and beautiful country," said Vancouver. "We will anchor and take on water and moose meat. Then in a week we shall set course for Hudson's Strait, Kap Farvel, and Ireland."

The men set about their busy ways, with a kind of unacknowledgeable satisfaction that they would in a few months see their own parishes. But they experienced another less happy feeling, a sort of early homesickness for the North Pacific Coast, a regret for the long coniferous shoreline with no man-made spires and no fences. In time this feeling of separation would pass, but for now they dreamed like men bewitched.

31

"I'm happier than you can imagine that you could come over tonight," said Don Juan.

The little supper that had been sent in, the Chinese and Mexican incense that Quadra habitually burned at eventide, the very excellent sherry, combined to fashion languor and then torpor.

"The duck was superb," said the younger man, "as is this Spanish wine.

"The English have always preferred our sherry to the French brandy. That is why you won Quebec rather than the Argentine."

Vancouver always felt so young when he was over here, so young and so well protected. He tried to think about Don Juan Quadra and James Cook. He had never felt protected by Cook; that was the beginning of a distinction. With Cook assuming the responsibility, he had dared to try his edge, to be if he could *ne plus ultra*. If Cook was a father he was the kind of father who would throw his son into the Atlantic to teach him to swim. If Don Juan was a father, he was a girl's father, warm, indulgent, ready to guide but more protective than boastful.

"We took Quebec because we are a nation of builders, of inventors, because we are industrious. The French must be either gentlemanly rulers in two-hundred-year-old carriages, or country clods, or effeminates in the expensive black skirts of the Italian church."

"My mother church," said Quadra.

"You are Spanish," said his protégé, "which means that you have the savagery of a Saracen disguised as a Catholic. You are no toadies to your parish priest. You burn your most unpopularly pious citizens, and create new varieties of Christianity in every land you bring under your dominion."

"I am not certain that the ways of your barbarians will not be more successful here in the North Pacific," said the Peruvian.

He offered Vancouver a pipe, but the latter demurred. Don Juan always liked to have a smoke and some political talk afterward. He was quite content during his last days at Nootka, even though he was for the first time during his command withdrawing from a region penetrated and possessed by Spanish skill.

"*My* barbarians?"

"Not yours personally. Though I do take you to be the type of a northern European officer. I mean the Russian traders who have established their vegetable churches in Alaska, and who have managed to float their ill-devised trading vessels as far south as this island. I mean your countryman, Meares . . ."

"He is no countryman of mine. He is a citizen of a land of lies! I get quite heated about him. Excuse me. I am sorry if I hurt you there."

"I assure you, Jorge, I am more delighted than hurt, though it did hurt. I like your heat. You are so much marked by it inside your disguise, and you so seldom permit one to feel it."

"If John Meares were to show up in Friendly Cove, he would feel it."

"But not in the manner that I have, surely, on the lucky occasion I've experienced."

"Of course not. May I have some more coffee?"

Quadra reached for the pot without getting up, and continued to talk while he poured out one cup of Blue Mountain coffee.

"Your John Meares is a poacher who hides behind a Portuguese flag, consorts with Yankee cross-palms, and hires Chinese to gut and denude dead animals in his ill-gotten factory here at Nootka. It was not alone to protect ancient Spanish rights to the Coast that Don Esteban José Martinez chased Meares away two years ago. It was to free this innocent landing, not yet protected by a mission, from ugliness and filth."

Vancouver could not help loving him. He would never denounce the villain in question in such terms, but they were the ones he wanted to use. He was a man who got to where he was going under his own watchful gaze. He drank the coffee. It was not as hot as it is at its best, but tepid it fell off his tongue with a true taste of the south, his second.

"You know, I should not tell you this, but Pitt the Younger said some unflattering things, too, about the Spanish navy. When he demanded the return of Nootka . . ."

"The relinquishment of Nootka, I think."

"He has designs to place people only marginally better than Meares in Nootka Settlement. He wants to bring convicts from New Holland and begin a colony of them along this coast."

Don Juan smiled and ran a moistened finger along his moustache.

"Do you find it interesting that the Spanish deposit their priests first upon the soil of new lands, while the British begin with their convicted prisoners?"

"It is perhaps because you papists deem the world

itself a prison, so what matters it where one serves his sentence? The fathers, of course, are despatched to the four corners to disabuse the tribesmen in those places of their fancy that they are free."

"There have been occasions, I will admit, when I have thought as much," said the elegant Don.

"I wonder, though, whether both Spanish priests and Irish prisoners might be pioneers to be preferred over the first Americans to meet any new natives, for those are nearly certain to be purveyors of rum and firearms."

"The which you have never provided for our dark-skinned brothers?"

"James Cook and my own moral discretion taught me never to trade either of those two commodities to aborigines. The Americans evidently are satisfied with the discovery that they bring furs more readily than any other prize. It is my hope that we become prepared at some time to defeat those pirates in a national war. I expect that we will not have to abide long until their first depredations against British territory and rights."

"We Spanish are on salutory terms with the Yankee, so far," said Don Juan, signalling by the restive movements of his body that the discussion was over.

"I'm not sure that you can use 'salutory' that way in English," said Vancouver, preparing to rise.

"In the Lord's language we say *salubre*."

"*Salud*."

"I will drink your health once more, and then you must retire to your own palace upon the main."

32

"What does the white man want?" asked the first Indian.

It was a friendly meeting, more or less, held on the slope just above the waterline at the edge of Cheslakees' village. Cheslakees was, next to Maquinna across the island, the main chief in these parts, around Johnstone's Straits. George Vancouver, along with some of his officers and Archibald Menzies, sat on skins placed over the ground. Puget was angry that he had been instructed to leave his specially constructed picnic chair in the tender. Vancouver did not want to place his contingent higher than the Red Men. He was a little surprised when Tyee Cheslakees arranged things so that the Indians were seated a little higher up the slope.

"They haven't said yet," said the second Indian. "So far they have just been going through their elaborate greetings and ceremonial preparations. We have learned not to rush them directly into business or they would feel insulted. The white man places great importance on saving as opposed to losing face."

The village was exposed to a southern aspect, whilst higher hills beyond, covered with lofty pines, sheltered it completely from the northern winds. The houses, in number thirty-four, were arranged in regular streets; the larger ones were the habitations of the principal people, who had them decorated with paintings and other ornaments, forming various figures, apparently the rude designs of fancy; though it is by no means improbable they might annex some meaning to the figures they described, too remote, or hieroglyphical, for our comprehension. The house of Cheslakees was distinguished by three rafters of stout timber raised above the roof, according to the architecture of Nootka, though much inferior to those in point of size. The whole, from the opposite side of the creek, presented a very picturesque appearance.

"A very handsome village, indeed," offered Vancouver, through his interpreter though he had nearly as much of the language himself. Protocol came and went, but to such a site it usually came.

"Thank you, we like it," said Tyee Cheslakees.

"I suppose you get a lot of rain in these parts," suggested Vancouver.

"Not so much in the summer," said the chief. "In the winter it rains all the time, but we always say that at least you don't have to shovel it."

"I could think of a good use for a shovel right now," whispered the first Indian.

Now the conversation came to a rest while the songs were performed. The first song was quite melodious, but it was accompanied by the most savage of gestures and grimaces. Peter Puget was seen to edge his hand closer to his formal sword. That is, he was seen by some of the white men and all the Indians. Then when that song was finished, all the officers were presented with strips of sea otter skin. This took some time, and was followed by the women's song. During the singing of this quieter but rhythmical piece, Vancouver spied Menzies, his eyes closed and his head bobbing up and down in time with the music.

"Very nice," said Vancouver. "I especially liked the last number."

"We are proud of our women's choir," said the Tyee, or so it came out in translation. "Just about every year they are the best on the island."

"Speaking of the island . . ." Vancouver let the phrase hang for a while.

"Here we go," muttered the second Indian.

"Yes?"

"Speaking of the island, I hear that some of your people have been off the island."

"Of course."

"I mean a good way off."

"That is a relative concept."

"Someone in Nootka told me, after I had explained my interest, that of all the people on the Coast, some of your people have been farther inland than anyone else."

"It's possible," said Cheslakees, and the interpreter allowed the same suggestive look to come into his own eyes.

Vancouver gestured to Whidbey, his ship's master, who removed the sacking from a package of objects, knives, axeheads, beads, Bibles, and Irish linen. These the Indians were supposed to look at. Vancouver felt his usual distaste. He would not have had the stomach to be a merchant. Goods, trade, pelf, he tried to forget that they would be the result of his explorations. Yet poets bartered sweet fashionings of the mind for a new suit of wool.

"You offer no muskets?" enquired the chief, but not with any great challenge in his voice. He did not want to forfeit his chance for these things, especially the linen.

"Trading in firearms is against my law," replied the commander.

"No matter," said Cheslakees. "I have eight muskets in my house. All Spanish."

With a smile on his lips, he waved his hand and two of his people stepped forward. One was middle-aged, the other a young man. Both appeared more than commonly healthful, with beautiful long muscles and the clear eyes the traveller associates with people who live on mountaintops.

"You may ask of these two," said the chief. "They are my most experienced sojourners and probably our most observant eyes."

"You have been a great distance inland?" asked the stout sailor of all the world's seas.

"It is a relative question," said the first Indian.

Vancouver did not realize that he was twisting the strip of sea otter skin in his hands, though all the Indians had seen it. He decided to come to the point.

"Far into the mountains and beyond them lies a great sea, as great as the sea that stretches west of this island."

The second Indian nodded his head in the white man's fashion.

"You know of it?" asked Vancouver, a pin of hot ice entering his stomach.

"Oh yes," said the second Indian. The first Indian remained impassive, the way Indians liked to do in front of white men, to suggest that they were patient.

"You have . . . seen it?" asked Vancouver at last.

"We have," said the second Indian.

Vancouver couldn't wait for the interpreter now. He leaned forward, his short wig slipping a little on his head. He addressed the young barbarian directly, in a rough estimation of the Nootka tongue.

"How through forest it days with canoes many is?"

Years later Benjamin Wharf would be built where this aching query was put.

"It is as many suns as we all have fingers on our

hands," said the second Indian, looking about as if to count by fives. "Many portage. Many days eating chickens on the flat land past the highest mountains."

This last was an inspired guess.

"Where is the entrance to your passageway?" asked Whidbey, unable to wait for his captain to put the question.

"It is the third broad inlet beyond the Rock of Ripples," said the young traveller.

Vancouver stared without movement for a few moments. Then he thanked the two travellers, he thanked the Tyee, he proceeded through the disengagememt ritual, and strode with filled chest to the boat, as a duet sang the song of the virgins. Then the Europeans were gone, past the mouth of the river, and into the fog.

The first Indian waited till they had walked some distance from the group who were trying on the Irish linen.

"Why did you tell him such things?" he enquired of his young friend. "We have never been farther than ten days into the interior."

"I saw that he had come to buy something," said his companion, "and all I had was a dream I remembered from last winter."

33

He had, this is true, dipped into Vancouver's journal for Johnstone's Straits, and come up with the word "fancy." It was like finding the Strait of Anian in Florence, and it was also like several other things, found. When he found those things he knew a book was going well, that is without oars, before a good wind. Or he could be forgiven for thinking so. At times like that one did not necessarily believe in magic or its practitioners, the gods; but at times such as those one knew it was happening to itself rather than waiting around for him to think of it.

"Did you notice something odd about the *Mamathni*?" asked the first Indian the next day.

Mamathni was the Nootka word for the Europeans. In the Chickliset tongue it meant "their houses move over the water." The Indians plied canoes just about as long as the *Chatham* but they had never conceived the notion of placing chairs and tables and beds in them. Of course in their circumnavigation of the watery globe, the Englishmen, as well, one supposes, as the Spaniards, the Russians, and the French, were accustomed to being called many varied and fanciful names. A hundred miles north of here they were called *Yets-Haida*, which translated as Iron Men, a way of calling them very rich, not quite gods, but certainly permitted by the gods a favoured position in life.

"Of course," replied the second Indian now. "One cannot help noticing many odd things about them. They have, for instance, a profusion of hair upon their faces, which suggests their relationship with beasts such as the bear and the wolf. Yet they have magic glasses that make the distance near."

"Well, I mean something more basic, something one has never noticed about any other distant tribes."

"They have, of course, that thin transparent skin. I remember many years ago or when I was even younger than you are now, my friends and I seized one of them and scrubbed him till the blood came. We thought they were painted pink, you see, as the northerners paint themselves grey. We got into serious trouble, but at least we found out. They are real inside and pink on the surface. It is perhaps as if their exterior skin has been removed from them, and they are compelled to face the world with their inner skin. How they must suffer in a cold wind! It is an explanation of why they wear those heavy garments covered with pieces of shining metal."

All the while these words were being said, the first Indian was fidgeting, his fingers and toes moving out of sequence, and his mouth slightly open. At last he was able to get some Nootka words in edgewise.

"In my own short lifetime I have seen over a hundred *Mamathni*. You have seen many more than I have. Our people have seen them every summer for twenty years at least."

"There are stories that our great grandfathers saw them. At least that is the most common interpretation these days of their stories about flame-bearded gods who sailed here from the sun."

The second Indian loved being middle-aged. It meant that he could be the one who passes on the stories from the old people to the young people, while still being able to pursue most of the young people's duties and pleasures. One also was credited with a certain store of wisdom. He thought he knew what his young friend was going to point out.

"What I would like to point out, if it has to be left to me," said the first Indian, "is that the *Mamathni* are all male."

That wasn't it. The second Indian was really taken aback. But it was true. There were boys on their houses that moved over the water, and there were men as old as himself. But there were no old men, and there were no females at all. It was a thought very difficult to assimilate.

"Now that you mention it, I see it. The pink people are all men. In that regard, the strangest race of people we have ever encountered. Nowhere else in nature have I ever met such a thing."

He was a truly disoriented middle-aged man for the moment.

"How do they make more of themselves, then?" asked the first Indian, as they sat on the rocks looking toward the cove where the buttoned people had last been seen.

"Perhaps they fall from the sky with the rain, as frogs do," said the second Indian.

"One of their number is often in the forest or the meadows, drawing pictures of plants, and taking plants to their floating house," said the lad. "Is it possible that they have in some way learned to mate with the plants to produce more of their kind?"

"Such a thing seems too fanciful for the imagination."

The second Indian was a little bashful for some reason, but he continued. "I have been thinking about it, and it seems to me that we should cleave to the simple line of reason."

"So you always say."

"Facts are facts."

"But the large wingèd craft on the sea bring us new facts in great numbers."

"Logic demands that we begin with these facts: the *Mamathni* are men, not gods; men like to fuck, but the *Mamathni* have no females in their species. Therefore, it seems plain that they fuck each other."

"Thus producing children?"

"So it would seem. You said yourself that their floating houses bring countless new facts. If a people can live with no permanently fixed home but rather houses that are nearly always in motion, they can probably produce children in their own way too."

The first Indian was playing with the scissors that had been part of the deal for the dream of the large eastern sea. He cut the leaves one by one from a salmonberry bush.

"We have our own men who like to fuck each other," he said at last.

"But they are not many. They are a minority, an exception to our ways. They are usually artists and designers and sometimes teachers. The *Mamathni* are presumably all that way."

"Maybe when men fuck men all the time it makes their skin turn pink."

"Maybe when men fuck men all the time they learn the lore that takes them great distances on wingèd homes filled with useful objects made of iron."

34

He rode his bicycle forty blocks down the hill to the credit union, where he paid the mortgage. Their large house was the only thing they had stationary on the earth. It was big and full of rooms and the rooms were full of things. In one of the rooms he sometimes tried to write a book. After he had been around the world he always came back to this house.

On his way back up the hill he had to get off and push his bike for a few blocks. The street was named after a tree by the time it passed their house, but along the steepest part, where he was pushing his bike in the cool-warm December air, it was named Puget Drive.

Peter Puget just plain hated the natives. Archibald Menzies spent days and nights with them as if they were any other foreigners who were half familiar and half strange. Zack Mudge, who could and did read French, was forever going on about "*le noble sauvage*," and so on. But Captain Vancouver had a number of varied reactions to them.

True, he had been struck athwart the head by a

paddle in the hands of a Sandwich Islander, and smacked unceremoniously into the waves while serving under James Cook. But the Spanish ruffians had more latterly performed a like operation in the Canaries, throwing his punched-up body into the Atlantic. Still, when they had been in the Sandwiches this most recent time, he'd been suspicious of the Islanders' intentions. When he was spilled from a native canoe into the surf at Oahu, he was certain that they were trying to kill him, even after they saw him rescue a drowning midshipman.

"Treacherous dogs," he muttered, pressing salt water out of his skirts.

"We should shoot a dozen of them, make our stay here a lot less complicated," put in Puget.

"You are too suspicious, captain," said Mr. Menzies. "It is because you learn their language in order to practise your control over them, while you never get close enough to them to listen to that language for a while and find out what they want."

Vancouver was about to remind the botanist that though a civilian he was still subject to the common discipline of the mission, but he had a distaste for thus repeating himself, and so desisted.

Instead he said, "I found out what they wanted in Tahiti. What they wanted chiefly was British property, including the uniforms at the time worn by the British sailors."

"Yes, and you had two Tahitian men, in front of their families and neighbours, shorn bald and flogged, for purloining one hat."

"That is correct, Mr. Menzies. We also have some of their hats, which we paid for, in trade. It is the way we British do it, sir. We are not, sir, a bunch of republicans."

But it was not only the discovered people who were to be lashed into shape. After the riot at Tenerife, he had had his own men flogged, cursing the Spanish every time the whip lapped loudly into the flesh. He was a contemporary of Captain Bligh. He ran a healthier ship, resorted to the lash less often, but maintained a better discipline than that of his famous rival. There were times, to be sure, when he was forced to his bed by physical and nervous exhaustion.

At Kauai, Peter Puget loaded his boat and asked the commander for permission to remain ashore till morning. Vancouver ordered him to run the surf by moonlight, and Puget lost a lot of equipment to the sea and the dark swimmers therein. Vancouver received the news, gave his further orders, and retired. In his bed he was attended by Menzies, who saw a hyperthyroid, and exophthalmic goitre a long way from home. He saw the next morning a captain standing at his rail displaying puffy eyes, a noticeably swollen throat, hypertension, and exhaustion.

"You must take to your bed, and pass command over to Mr. Mudge," said the surgeon. "At least for a week. And eliminate salt from your diet."

"Is that a facetious remark, sir?"

"No, sir; a physician's sound advice."

It still smacked of wordplay and sarcasm to the commander, and no wonder.

"Give me a compound and begone," he said. "Or I will have *you* flogged."

"Not me, sir, replied Menzies.

The next day Menzies observed his patient shouting at their carpenter, Henry Phillips. It became apparent that the carpenter had dared to suggest to Vancouver that he, Phillips, knew more about making a new foretopgallant yardarm than the captain did. For this opinion he was shouted at, arrested, confined, sent home, and three and one-half years later court-martialled on the strength of a deposition left by the late commander.

When the two boats became separated during the exploration of the fingers leading from Burrard Inlet, Thomas Manley, the twenty-two-year-old master's mate, took his boat back to the ship after running out of provisions. When Vancouver returned a day later he delivered a vicious diatribe to the young man, in front of a few officers.

Later Manley was able to speak, and he said to Menzies, who was engaged in watering his plants: "His salutations I can never forget, his language I will never forgive unless he withdraws his words by a satisfactory apology."

"Don't hold your breath," said Menzies.

35

The end of the summer was miserable and disappointing and exhausting. At first Vancouver had been happy when the Spanish captains Valdes and Galiano agreed to join their two little ships and crews to his two ships as they travelled from Birch Bay north, to become the first international surveying team. They supplied one another with copies of their charts made thus far, and proceeded up the coast. Vancouver visited the small Spanish schooners, and noticed that while the accommodations for officers were lavish, the guns were few, and working areas well supplied but underdeployed.

Soon Vancouver ran into the difficulty he usually had with people outside his jurisdiction: no one had the superstitious or logical drive to be as thorough as he was. The serrated coastline here was singularly difficult of measurement and description. Puritan Vancouver and his Protestant crew rowed doggedly, dropped chain again almost as soon as it was pulled from the water. Their thoroughness made charts to be employed by international helmsmen two centuries into the future. The Spaniards, on the other hand, were more relaxed, as they might say, more leisurely, said Vancouver. Often one of them would venture an estimate and another would endow it with the authoritativeness of black India ink.

It was not long before the British and the Spanish leaders entered into the first of a number of squabbles concerning methods and expectations.

"Excuse me if I appear to misapply my art, but if the bottom is eleven feet from the surface, I like to know it. I do not want to possess a chart that presumes twelve feet. Especially in the event that I am in a vessel that is drawing eleven feet of water."

Dionisio Galiano offered his British opposite number a silver box of snuff, and when Vancouver refused with half the politeness called for, took a pinch himself, delaying his reply long enough to ensure his own enjoyment of a maximum advantage to be extracted from the rhythm and the rhetoric.

"Eleven feet, twelve feet," he said at last. "These are only facts, captain. Facts are a fine basis upon which to gauge the amount of cabbage to stuff into your hold, but you must not take too lightly the experienced and successful sailor's other great friend, his imagination. You must use your imagination."

"*My* imagination?"

"A problem in switching from one language to the other," said Cayetano Valdes. "Captain Galiano means of course to say that *one* must use *one's* imagination."

He too sniffed the powder far up into his nasal passages.

Privately George Vancouver was now thinking about how easily the word imagination tripped off a Catholic tongue. That ease seemed to be connected somehow with the flashy Iberian uniforms and the silver and gold of the dinner service in the tiny dining room here aboard the *Sutil*.

Silver and gold. The shores of the Northwest Passage would be sprinkled with those two metals.

"The imagination," he said. "You speak of it as if it were the opposite of facts, as if it were perhaps the enemy of facts. That is not true in the least, my two young friends. The imagination depends upon facts, it feeds on them in order to produce beauty or invention, or discovery. The imagination is never the enemy of my eleven feet. The true enemy of the imagination is laziness, habit, leisure. The enemy of imagination is the idleness that provides fancy."

The Spanish surveyors and the British surveyors agreed on this evening to split up and go their ways, to produce alternate maps or duplicate ones, as the eventualities might occur. Vancouver had been planning for some time to make his own charts of the coastline already surveyed by the Spaniards in any case.

The more it rained the more was Vancouver's body tormented. His throat was so much swollen and painful that ofttimes he could not swallow any of the plain English food brought to him. He coughed continuously, and sometimes pink frothy blood came up with the sputum. His chest was sore on any day upon which it was not clear and bright and warm, and as August appeared those days grew fewer. It was an unusually rotten summer on the West Coast. Still Vancouver drove himself hard, as if he had a wife and family to support.

Then in the late afternoon of August 6, H.M.S. *Discovery* caught a rock and stuck as the tide ran out. The stern fell into the deep water while the bow rose right out of the sea. Then the whole thing began to fall over sideways, as the water grew ever more shallow ahead. It looked as if the ship that had come more than halfway round the world was going to slide off the rock, stern first into the deep Pacific.

The *Chatham* anchored out of reach of the shoals,

and sent out all boats filled with men to help the desperate crew of the distressed bark. They hauled upon the stream anchor until it tore loose from its housing. Then the tops of the masts with their yard-arms were hauled down and fashioned into props which men would attempt to plunge into the water that wanted to float them away from the listing ship.

Meanwhile the sailors were trying to keep their footings on the sloped decks, as fresh water, fuel and ballast were cast overboard to keep her as light as possible. The boats were overfilled with supplies, and set floating. The listing continued till the bulwarks were two and a half inches from the drink. The sea was amazingly, as if magically, calm. Even moderate waves now would have doomed the rescue. The *Discovery* was likely to run suddenly under the ocean.

At nine that night, with the sun low over the water, the ebb tide was at its lowest. Men stood in water to their waists and applied the last of the props. The least vital of the supplies were thrown to the fish. After midnight the water began to rise, and to the wonderment of Vancouver's people, but to his apparent expectation, the vessel slowly began to right itself. At 2:30 in the morning they heaved so that the unbroken hull floated again. The frantic and exhausted men, jubilant but nearly dead from tension and fear and ceaseless work, threw themselves upon their faces to sleep like dead men.

Three hours later they were awake and working again. The ship must be reprovisioned, the boats emptied and put away, fuel and water and ballast collected ashore and the ship refitted for the run past the rocks and to the open sea during high tide. At one o'clock in the afternoon they picked up a light breeze and ran before it for five miles. Then the breeze fell away to dainty gusts and finally nothing. The ships again floated without aim on the ebb tide. At six o'clock the *Chatham* ran into some rocks hidden just below the surface. The *Discovery* sent off all its boats and men, near corpses kept on the move now only by a crazed end-of-the-world curiosity.

Once again they were compelled to work all night, unloading the ship, propping it up, desperately trying to keep poles between it and the bottom as the swells banged it against the rocks. But there were just not enough spars and yards to do the job. Miraculously, it seemed, the tide running out the channel brought them some driftwood, and it was just sufficient to save their ship. The hysterical sailors said curses and shouted prayers as they put props dangerously in place and rode out the midnight, till on the returning tide, at one in the morning, the *Chatham*, its hull unbroken, floated free.

Again the morning was given to restocking and stowing the vessel. Then for two days they ran the channel, the demented sailors watching the waters splash around the rocks that protruded everywhere and promised other rocks just below the surface. But they found the open sea at last, and in the end-of-summer's rain, did another week's surveying in Fitzhugh Sound.

There they met the East Indian fur trader *Venus*, that had come over the foam from Nootka, with a letter for George Vancouver. It was from the supply ship *Daedalus*. Her commander, Richard Hergest, had been Vancouver's best friend. The letter announced that Richard had been murdered in Hawaii.

Vancouver could not send his boats out again. He rolled his charts, stowed his equipment, set the officers to correcting and tidying their logs, and sailed for Friendly Cove, where Bodega y Quadra was to be waiting to hand over control of the Nootka Station.

36

Coming to love was difficult for the commander; it was perhaps not as long a voyage, but a stranger one, than coming to command. He had put off sailing to Nootka because, he told himself, and there is some justification, surely, for doing so, the coastline north was long and complicated, and the summer short. Nootka could be achieved on the way to the Sandwich Islands. Simply.

Coming to Nootka was something a little embarrassing, and this was because of who and what he is. Is.

The power of Spain over the bend of the planet's oceans was ebbing after these centuries, and the force of Britain was still expanding. It reached out with Vancouver to limn the unknown edges of the remaining land masses, while Spain had begun to collapse inward, leaving Quadras at the perimeter to tidy up and salute the succeeding Britishers.

He would have to be very polite to the Spaniard.

These two seemed to be the types of their respective national conditions. Vancouver was informed that he would be receiving control from a man of about fifty years, who would be resplendent in the Iberian way, but so much enfeebled that if the fancy metal on his uniform were suddenly removed he would crumple to the floor. Vancouver did not believe that for a second because he was of the opinion that a man who had achieved command of a whole coast had to boast the strength of no ordinary mortal. Still, here he was, comparatively a youth, preparing to accept a European-made submission from a man as old as James Cook.

Coming to this meeting abashed him somewhat because the man he was sailing to meet was of a noble Spanish family, though they did have a lot more noble families in their population than did the English. They were like the Italians that way. It was more in the way of a distinction to be a nobleman in England after all, so Vancouver was made by himself aware of his own origins in the civil service. But at the same time he could not, as a European, renounce his feelings of superiority over a man who had been born in South America, even though his birth had happened fifteen years before his own.

Which thought unnerved him even more, because the Spanish Crown and the Spanish admiralty were not in the habit of conferring the highest appointments in their possessions to men who had been born in those possessions, even if the parents were of the most impeccably white nobility. Señor Don Juan Francisco de la Bodega y Quadra must have been one hell of a naval officer.

On those grounds Vancouver felt himself secure; it was only when he thought about his middling Protestant birth and his social conduct shaped by the war-immanent sea that he began to panic a little, imagining a dozen ways to avoid Nootka. His worst fear, or the one imagined most visually, was that the Spanish gentleman would meet him with horses, and his nervousness and incapacity concerning those beasts would be discovered to all.

Outside the palace, William Blake's companion, Thomas Taylor, said to his silent friend, "You must endeavour to understand the king's violent reaction to your drawings. He is a man whose attention since childhood has been given to the shaping and maintenance of the Empire."

"The sword has been known to sleep in his hand."

"What I mean to say, Blake, is that the king does not understand art."

Blake smiled the kind of smile a person who is supposed to be a sage or artist will smile when he wants to indicate that he himself has been reminded of a knowledge he has long retained though it might still stay hidden from you.

"Yes, he does," he said. "He sees it clear. He understood the drawings at once, and that is why he shouted what he did."

As always his friend wondered whether Blake were mystifying the occasion, averring something about a world we normal eighteenth-century souls could not follow, or whether he were as mad as a button maker.

When he found out that Don Juan could speak English while he himself knew no Spanish, he knew himself completely outclassed, and gave himself in to that entirely, for the older man had been thoughtful enough to employ an interepreter when they were conversing in public.

On the other hand, in their most private and brutish moment he had called him the most vile of names, in English, loudly and directly into his ear.

He had sailed twenty thousand miles with his eyes

peeled to espy what they all might be; and now with his eyes shut tight he knew what he was.

In the next few days Quadra politely informed Vancouver that he had been sailing about these waters since he was a boy, and that the post taken away from Meares was a Spanish property regained from pirate hands. All his life Nootka had been Spain's northernmost community, and he could not accept a newcomer's view that it was British. Vancouver just as diplomatically conveyed the information that his mission was to receive the post in consequence of a pact signed in Europe by their respective governments, and that he was of no mind to confuse that fact with the economic history of the region.

After sundown they never discussed the letters that went back and forth between them during the day. They told each other tales of the sea, and compared their disdains for French sailors, Chinese and Indian food, and Yankee traders. Like women, they offered each other the services of their respective surgeons. Dr. Rodriguez told Vancouver he had gout and that he should refrain from eating sauerkraut. Dr. Menzies cured Don Juan of a headache he had suffered with grace for two years.

"I will give you Nootka and all the coast as far south as California, if you will give me your surgeon," said the happy Peruvian one evening.

He was surprised to see Vancouver's two eyes look out at him through a veil of pain and disgust and disappointment. The man was English and Protestant, but he contained complexities no portrait painter had ever allowed a man in a Royal Navy tunic.

37

Menzies kept the carcass of that brown albatross around for weeks, and some of the officers made faces and some of the men were heard to mutter unpleasant words. But he was the scientist, and therefore up to something they didn't understand, so they had to put up with it.

Not that they were superstitious about the albatross. They didn't give two hoots about an albatross. Unless there was a literary person about. If there was a literary person about, they let on about how the great spread albatross over the quarterdeck was the source of supernatural calm, and the dead albatross was a source of the supernatural dread. Once when there was a German poet stalking around the vessel while they were tied up at Capetown, a sailor named Delsing told him that he had once as a lad thrown a belaying pin at a perching albatross, killing the bird on the spot. The older sailors, he told the German poet, had seized him and compelled him to wear the albatross around his neck untill it dropped off. But the sailors who overheard the telling of this tale doubled over with their sun-browned hands clapped over their mouths, the universal gesture executed by people who are trying not to laugh or throw up.

The truth of the matter was that you could never throw a belaying pin straight enough to hit an albatross, and if you did, you could never throw it hard enough to kill him. If you managed to get him the pin would bounce off him and fall onto the deck, and the albatross would look at it there, then look over at you, and then look away again and stand up on tiptoe, flap his long jointed wings, and jump away into the breeze.

That's why everyone was deeply impressed when the little botanist Menzies brought down the bird with a second shot from his flintlock pistol.

So it was not that they were superstitious. If they had been superstitious, and especially if there had been a literary person on board, they might have looked at the decaying bird and said things such as:

"I don't like it."

"It makes me uneasy."

"It's an unholy thing he is doing."

"No good can come of it."

"We shall be paying for his affront, mark my words."

"I fear him and his glittering eye."

But it wasn't superstition at all that fetched their disapprobation. It was a normal distaste for the ongoing apparition of a large dead and decaying bird on the premises. On board a ninety-nine-foot ship one cannot comfortably imagine the rotting body a great enough distance from the cook's supply of salt beef. The rumour that they were putting saltpetre in the mashed potatoes was bad enough. So what they were actually saying, historically but nonliterarily, was more like this:

"Aw, shit. I don't see why we have to put up with this from a civilian."

"Christ, I left Birmingham to get away from stinks like this."

"I feel like kicking that piece of shit over the side, and him after it."

"He's a Scot, and a Scot will eat a sheep's old stomach full of horse food, so it bothers him not at all; but I am a tender boy from West Sussex, and my nature was not formed for an outrage the like of this."

"Ah, you've got goose shit for brains!"

Thus were the minds of common British sailors unable for long to stay upon the same subject. But one memory was emblazoned now in their minds' eyes. That was the little fellow bringing down a bird near his own size, with a pistol more ornamental than dangerous in its appearance.

It was a device with a single flint and a small pan. Originally one of a pair, its mate was in a museum in Copenhagen. Menzies had been given this one as a present from Mr. Banks, on the occasion of his appointment aboard the *Discovery*.

Its furniture was gilt brass, heavily applied and cast with designs of scrollwork and classical heads in relief. Its brass lock plate was engraved with scrollwork. The long barrel was chiselled with strapwork and a classical figure, and bore the mark of Daniel Thiermay. Thus it may have been of French make, and if so the only object of French manufacture aboard Captain Vancouver's ship. In any case the ornamental weapon was fashioned in about 1725, and was, nearly seventy years later, in excellent condition.

Actually there had been not only another pistol but also a gun, decorated *en suite*, all bearing the mark of Daniel Thiermay. The gun disappeared after its last discharge against the British at Gibraltar, and was probably lying beneath the deep waters of the Bay.

On some of Thiermay's pieces his name is followed by the phrase, *à Paris*. But the Thiermay family is known to have operated in Liège, where brass mounts of the type found on Menzies' flintlock were especially popular. Some suthorities there conjecture that Daniel Thiermay worked in Liège but signed his work *à Paris* to render it more saleable. But in that nothing definite is known of his career, it is not untoward to believe that he worked for a while at least in the French capital. So Menzies' beautiful and fated pistol may have known a French birthplace after all. It is a small irony in a large ocean.

In any case, when Archibald Menzies stepped out and aimed his barrel at the hovering albatross, a lot of seamen stopped what they were doing and watched him. Vancouver himself watched with a faint smirk from way up at the forecastle. Menzies just continued what he was doing, as if no one were around to make him self-conscious. He was neither superstitious nor impatient.

There was a flash and a bang and some smoke, and then there was the botanist shaking more powder into his pan and there was the albatross, which hadn't so much as singed a wing. Then there was a flash and a bang and some smoke, and the albatross hit the deck chin first with a clatter, and though the gathered sailors did not offer a clapping of hands, they did send up a murmuring that is universally recognized as applause.

Though George Vancouver did not offer Mr. Menzies a congratulatory word on his marksmanship, he did remember the utter lack of expression on his surgeon's face as the dead creature slammed to his planks.

38

Two nights ago he'd told a student of literature that he thought that imagination implied a travelling, or a trip. He meant not to use the latter word, or intended its use not at all in the lightsome way teenagers spoke of drugs or new religions or simply recent interests. Such usage is a nuisance, it is a ritualizing of a mutiny.

He said that a passive leaning on a rail and seeing what the coast provides for one's gaze is linear, foppery and fancy. Going there and looking, turning over a rock or a clam, that is what is meant by the imagination. The ship is the vessel of metaphor, a carrying across as they say.

Full of theory and baffled, he felt his brain settle down on the soft end of its stem. The volcanic mountains inland but visible from the main, received their new names without protest. The rhythm of the sentences seemed to call for more.

The Catholics murdered them by the thousands, sacked their cities, defiled their holy places, erased their alphabets, melted down their gold, and brought half-breeds upon their women. But somehow the Catholics made greater inroads into the lives of the Indians than any Protestant, explorer, conqueror, or settler, ever did. The Iroquois and the Aztecs became part of the global village that is the Catholic church at its rites, but one would look far and wide before coming upon a Redskin who professed to be a Nonconformist, much less an Anglican.

At Nootka, the great native chief Maquinna was fond of the Spaniards, and fond of visiting them. For him the dinner table of Don Juan Quadra was the symbol of *Mamathni* behaviour. He was also proud, and as far as the whites were concerned, pride was a very important quality in the Indian. He was proud of the trust the strong and wise foreigners had in him. There was never any question of armament when he and his entourage visited the Spanish ships, nor when Quadra and his boatload of people disembarked at Maquinna's village. The West Coast, in this regard, was the image of peacefulness.

But Maquinna made the same mistake about the White Men Without Women as the latter often made about the various sorts of brown people: he thought they were all alike. So one day shortly after the British ships had anchored at Friendly Cove he caused himself to be transported to the *Discovery*, where he planned to greet the new visitors to the Coast.

"Hold it right there!" said the sentry on duty.

He didn't exactly aim his musket at the stout native standing among the paddlers in his dugout. But he wasn't exactly presenting arms, either.

"My name is Maquinna, chief of chiefs in these parts, and I come to make pleasantries with your chief," said Maquinna.

Unfortunately, he spoke only Nootka, with a smattering of Halkomelem and Spanish. The sentry was a twenty-one year old named Andrew Macready from Glasgow. He had trouble understanding what the English officers said, so it is no wonder that all he perceived was a sort of fat Indian saying something like, "*Euclatle muh Maquinna, kimscutla naw kimscutla, neah kyumkhwaltek Nootka skaw kimscutla koakoax*."

In any event he wasn't having any of it.

"Get tha' goon, ye doorty savage!" he replied, perhaps brandishing the musket in the direction of the chief of chiefs.

"He just looked like a regular heathen. How was I supposed to know he was a chief?" the young Macready was later to enquire of the officer in charge of his flogging.

Whatever the truth, one may be sure that Maquinna wasted no time in going to vent his unhappy feelings before his good friend Juan Quadra.

"I am not accustomed to having my dignity mishandled so easily," he told the Spanish commandant.

"Of course not," said the latter. "But we must both seem at least to be a bit more patient with the English. They are without gods, and therefore ignorant when it comes to conversing with those into whose heads the gods still speak."

"This poor coastal chief finds it difficult to understand what is meant by a people without gods. Who is it, then, that instructs them during moments of great decision?"

"It is a phenomenon called human consciousness," said Quadra. "Their chief, Mr. Vancouver, has a great deal of it."

"Yet they have sailed their wingèd canoes past many lands, you tell me. The world is becoming a different place too rapidly for this peaceful chief."

Quadra, as was his wont, told Maquinna as much as he could about the English, to explain to him why he had been treated as he had; then he told Vancouver what a mistake had been made aboard his ship. He told him further how to patch things up. So Vancouver had eight presents dispatched to the chief, along with a humble and importunate invitation to break fast aboard the *Discovery* upon the morrow.

Breakfast went along fine for a while. Quadra complimented Vancouver upon the fish. Maquinna was so well dressed that no one, from Glasgow or elsewhere, could mistake him for less than a great political personage.

But Peter Puget did not like him. He did not like the idea of a red savage sitting at the captain's board and placing the captain, as he saw it, on the defensive. To give some course to his resentment, he kept refilling Maquinna's glass with claret.

Meanwhile the sun had risen high over the island's mountains, and laid generous light over everything on the sea, the way it does in the morning at Trieste. Some of it came through an opened shutter and pierced its way into Maquinna's red cut-glass goblet.

"No," he said, and was dutifully translated. "No, you English do not know how to conduct yourselves when you are in the presence of a people's leaders. These Spanish now, they are gentlemen. Their wine is also of superior quality."

"I'll cut off his badges of authority and feed them to the crows," said Puget in an aside. He worked on the assumption that asides were not translated.

Maquinna said that the greatest sadness in his life was about to come down because the Spanish were leaving. He said that he was afraid that the British would probably eventually hand him over, along with his lands and people, to the Yankees. He had hated the Yankees ever since the time when he was standing in front of Meares' skin store and a Yankee sailor had stuck a cigar in his mouth. He was a pipe smoker for one thing, and the Yankee had laughed at him for another.

Here was an opportunity for Quadra, if he were so inclined, to drop the seeds of trouble between English and Nootka. Instead, he told Maquinna on his honour as a Spaniard that the chief could expect continuing decent treatment by the Europeans. Vancouver looked intently at the chief's face, and saw that he was thoroughly convinced. Then he looked at Quadra's face, and was chilled and excited by what he saw there.

That night the Peruvian was cruel and then he was more kind that he need be.

Part Three

The Dead Sailors

39

Europe has been building for a thousand years, and the people there have made their choice of what to keep. In the Americas the Indians would have begun to do that, but they were interrupted, so they said in their new language, Ah shit! Here in Guatemala de la Asunción they are to be found sitting on narrow sidewalks, as close to the storefront wall as possible, and they all look very patient.

He had gone east to Trieste because the Europeans had come west, and now he was going south to Guatemala because they had come north. They had come north in the summer, and he was going south in the winter. He did not know, to be sure, why all this, but he trusted it, though as the voyage grew longer and the book got thicker he felt himself resting more and more on his faith in the readers: would they carry him, keep him afloat? He thought so. The B-747 filled to capacity with people and baggage, touched the earth like a giant bird touching down on the sea.

The breakfast had not rendered things perfect between Vancouver and Maquinna, but it had made things better than they had been the night before, thanks mainly to Don Juan's advice and explanations.

A few days later Maquinna and his company departed to his royal village at Tahsis. Once again Quadra gave his valuable advice to his young friend. The white men should make a ceremonial visit to the native ruler. Immediately it came into Vancouver's mind that the idea was an example of Spanish Catholic foolishness, the love of ostentation that an English Protestant felt did not become him. But he remembered that his teacher had been right about everything save Spanish-English politics so far, and he imagined also the practical good that might come of such a visit. Then of course he saw that the Peruvian had thought of that years ago.

So he dressed his marines in their scarlet uniforms, caused the cutter to be painted new, and beneath a bright sun they set out, Vancouver, Quadra, and some of their officers in the cutter, with others crowded into three other boats. They were red, white, and blue on the water; they were gold and brass under the late summer sun. Up the long narrow inlet they plied water like a looking glass.

The natives came toward them in their long dugout canoes, solemnly but in a peaceful fashion, saluting the over-dressed foreigners. Vancouver gave the signal, and the marine drums and flutes played the first European military tunes ever heard in Tahsis Inlet. The bright sound echoed off the steep mountains so close on either side.

Thus they arrived before the seat of Maquinna. Vancouver had his men perform their snappiest landing procedure, then with the other officers ranged behind him, and Quadra at his side, he removed his sword and raised it to his eyes and his gold-rimmed hat. Quadra had suggested removing the hat, but the British commander was having none of that. Mr. Puget had been heard saying something rude in the back of the boat, but it was, as usual, ignored.

Maquinna was highly pleased anyway. The salute with the glittering sword, on top of the scarlet tunics and the lively drill, had established him before his people as an important personage. At least that is how Vancouver saw it.

The way Maquinna saw it, they were having a big party anyway, and the showy arrival of the *Mamathni* was in the order of entertainment. It was his eldest daughter Thia's birthday, her arrival at womanhood, and a time of requisite joy. She was receiving in her ceremonial outfit at her father's lodge, and thereto the officers filed to be greeted and favourably impressed by the princess. She was as gracious as any princess the Spanish and English gentlemen had ever seen, and no heavier.

"You are a fortunate man and an honoured father, Your Highness," said Don Juan Quadra through his interpreter.

"You deserve the envy of all men here," said the unmarried George Vancouver.

"I am twice honoured that you have said so," replied the smiling father.

"I wouldn't mind . . ." began Peter Puget, but he stopped short at an angry glance from Vancouver, and a second from Dr. Menzies.

"Come, let us proceed to the feasting and the dancing," said the chief of chiefs, and they all promenaded down the grassy slope to the great sward, where the Spanish sailors had prepared a formidable meal from the sumptuous viands and wines that Quadra always made a part of his important meetings. Not to be outdone, Maquinna's cooks supplied baked salmon and steamed clams and soapberry cordial.

After the banquet, complete with loud toasts, the furniture was cleared away and the dancing and singing began. First the Nootkas displayed their energetic war dances, and birthday dances, with wooden bird masks, and knees lifted high. Even the old man jumped and stamped until perspiration rolled off every part of his head and body. Then the unbending Vancouver had his sailors sing some lusty songs and sound their instruments and perform some reels and a dust-raising hornpipe. After much shouting and applause, and a last round of drinks, the Europeans bade their opposites goodnight and bivouacked near the shore. The next morning they were escorted by hungover but singing braves to the opening of the narrow inlet.

Vancouver slept most of the way home, his large round head resting upon Quadra's upholstered shoulder.

40

Once you have gone from continent to continent, then to isolated island, there is a great deal of boredom on a small ship. Seeing the same male faces every day for several years aboard a vessel only ninety-nine feet long (or sixty) can lead to unpleasant experiences. Antipathies among crew members are bound to develop after the most trivial events, a joke gone wrong, or a sock gone missing. Of course in addition to seeing the faces you would rather forget, you have to put up with the odours created and mixed by one hundred and one men, most of them English, ranged along those ninety-nine feet.

"If you don't wash your hair, mate, it's going to walk off your head, and I don't cherish having its vermin resettling in my kip."

"They wouldn't come near you, Sharkey. The stench of your feet would keep a killer alligator away."

"How would you like me to throw you and your passengers over the fucking side, you popish bastard?"

From which juncture that conversation took a theological turn.

The officers, needless to say, never engaged in such repartee, but you may be certain that they felt some various dislikings one for another. Zachary Mudge got along with everyone excepting Peter Puget, whose attitudes toward any one non-British got on his nerves. With the exception of Captain Vancouver, Mudge may have been the only man aboard the *Discovery* who did not have sex with the Tahitians and Indians. But he thought of them as people who were nearly as respectable as European Christians.

Aboard such a small vessel everyone was able to acquire intimate knowledge of the habits of everyone else; and this included the habits of the commander. So no one was in the dark concerning the feelings between Vancouver, for instance, and Quadra. Or to cite an equally interesting example, the feelings between Vancouver and Menzies. These had begun to be apparent from the beginning of the voyage, and were manifested in a variety of ways in the following years. Sometimes when Menzies happened to take his meals at the captain's table, Vancouver spoke to him with insulting politeness. When Menzies shot the albatross he was watched by Vancouver from a distance, and the commander was seen to sneer when he missed the first shot, then sneer again when he brought the bird down. Vancouver had an excellent face for sneering; it was round and puffy and nearly without colour, above a negligible neck. Next to Bligh, he was the best sneerer among his peers.

Of course the source of the coolness between the two men was complex, but it involved the definition of work and worthwhile activity aboard a military vessel. Vancouver, as was to be expected, wanted to be in the Atlantic or the Caribbean, sinking French ships; yet here in the North Pacific he proved his officers and crew the best explorers, navigators and map makers in the world. Menzies, for his part, was more interested in extending the limits of human knowledge about life than he was in ending it; so he was not averse to cutting into a body to explore and map that shore, even if once in a while he had to end the life of a flying or crawling exemplar.

Perhaps somewhere inside themselves the career navy man and the botanist admitted that their tasks were models for each other, but on the surface of the sea or the land they got along no better than an uppity Scot and a stuck-up Limey.

So at dinner Vancouver said, "Mr. Menzies, would you care for some of this excellent coconut, or are you grieving because you could not take it back with you to plant in the king's gardens?"

Feeling a little testier than usual this evening, Menzies remained polite but somewhat piqued, and replied, "I will have some, to be sure, but I sympathize with your regret that you had to cut the ball open whilst you would rather have kept it for the large gun in the case a republican man-of-war might show over the azimuth."

"Oh no, sir. If that unlucky event should transpire I shall have you protect us with your venerable hand weapon."

The officers laughed appreciatively at this salvo, and it was understood that while the commander had won the day, the civilian had made a good showing of his wit. When the Spanish brandy was brought out, Vancouver raised a glass to Menzies and nodded his head lightly, and Menzies returned the salute.

Such was the gentlemen's version of the exchange cited earlier between the two seamen.

Still, while it was not uncommon on board His Majesty's ships for seaman to kill seaman, such violence had never eventuated on the *Discovery*. In discussion over this fact, Mr. Mudge once averred that it was due to the fact that Vancouver had decided to sail without a chaplain in his entourage. No one agreed readily with such cynicism, but everyone more or less understood Mudge to be the wisest man in their company. While the others chuckled good-naturedly in response to his witticism, Menzies said something in Greek that nobody followed or quite heard.

That night Menzies worked long hours by the light of the moon, introducing nutrients of his own combination into the soil under his favourite specimens. Seeing him there, Zack Mudge stopped to share a pipe with him, something he took pleasure in doing once in a while.

"You know why he signed no churchman, do you not?" said the first lieutenant at his desired moment.

"'He is the central figure in his own faith," replied the botanist.

"While you are no believer?"

"I respect his skill and the animus that drives him."

"Judas might have said as much."

"You know I am no hanged man."

"So you follow."

"So we all follow. His skill and his energy lead us to the heads of a thousand inlets. He fancies that he will lead us out of this desert in the Northwest Passage and we will be with him that day in the promised land. Even if his exposure to the cold rains brings about his death."

"Is that your medical prognosis, doctor?"

Menzies tapped out his pipe.

"I hope that I will not be considered a mutineer or an infidel, but I cannot consider this place a desert," he said.

41

"Tomorrow," said Don Juan Quadra, "I will be sailing for San Francisco, and you will have begun to forget me."

It was the usual fear or complaint of the older man. Given the political situation, and the fact that they were anchored on the unseen western edge of the world, one should not expect more than that, the few months since they'd first seen each other, the few weeks anchorage at Friendly Cove. If this short time had been fantasy, the fact of California and old age was quick to follow. If this had been some form of truth, the Spanish commander was preparing to enter the long dream alone.

"I shall never begin to forget you," said the other man.

"When your Admiralty requests that you report to them about negotiations with the recent enemy, you will find yourself declaring in favour of King George and against Quadra."

"That will never happen. I will recount the friendship and cooperation that has characterized all our dealings here. On my charts these islands will bear the names of your officers."

The Peruvian gentleman reached for Vancouver's hand and held it between the two of his for a while before he spoke. When he did it was in quiet, slow English.

"What we have known is friendship and cooperation, yes. *Claro*, and dignity, honour, and decency. Yet any two diplomats might, if they were very lucky, find a similar relationship. We have known something far more precious, far more singular. It was as if on the face of the earth or the sea for the first time . . ."

"For me it was the first time," said the Englishman huskily.

Quadra squeezed the hand and urged: "We must find a way to commemorate what we have found. You could, if you are not afraid of the reaction by the patriots in your Parliament, name some small part of this Anian's Land after us, putting our names at least together for ever. The gentlemen in your Parliament could be told that the name is a monument to friendship and cooperation."

Immediately Vancouver freed his hand from the warm grip of the Spanish palms, and slowly swung his arm in a great circle. Then he looked into the reflecting eyes of his friend and said that this largest island off the whole west coast would be called the Island of Quadra and Vancouver.

So it was marked on the British charts.

But business, among gentlemen, is business. Vancouver could not take over the administration of Nootka upon Don Juan's terms, because they were less advantageous to the British than the Nootka Agreement had called for. As for that, said Quadra, he had heard nothing of this Nootka Agreement. The two agreed to send to Europe for further instructions. In the morning after their last meal and last long talk alone together, the commander of all the Spanish ships on the west coast of North America floated out on the tide and made for Monterey.

Vancouver may have been a man of honour and all that entails, but there was a depression of feeling on board the *Discovery* and the *Chatham*. The crew, and even some of the officers, had been all primed to take over the port of Nootka, and get busy setting up housekeeping. Vancouver was always very strict about his people's taking gifts or trade to the natives or entering their homes, though he and Broughton were doing those things regularly. But it was his custom to allow women to live aboard the ships while they were at anchor. Of course there was a lot of fucking, quite a few pregnancies and, especially in Tahiti, rampant venereal disease, because the French navy under Etienne Marchand had reached haven there some time before the arrival of the British.

But now the man they sometimes liked to refer to as the Norfolk Nit was sticking on a point of honour, and there was to be no domestic scene here till at least next summer. A few of the men gave each other the French disease, a few more beat on each other's heads, and most of them, as there was no real reason to bathe, gave up the practice even though they were not on the high seas.

"Damn it, sailor, get thee downwind of me, or I will throw this sauerkraut down the front of your blouse, do you hear me plain?"

" 'Pon my soul, I'll not be sitting downwind of you till the wind be filled with jasmines and roses otherwise. Why, just yestermorn I saw a gull fall dead from the rail into the salt, and all from perching downwind of you."

The first sailor threw his sauerkraut down the front of the second sailor's blouse. He was, unfortunately for him, observed in this act by Captain Vancouver, who had been standing amidships, staring in the direction that the Spanish barks had gone two days before. He was, as we have seen, a fanatic about sauerkraut and discipline. He ordered for the first man twenty lashes, and for the second man ten.

42

Life aboard such small ships could be very boring indeed. If they were on the deep sea, one horizon looked much like another. If they were at surveying, a man might look from the ship to the same scrap of shoreline day after day, with no strange people within hundreds of miles, the only animal the quiet oyster. Or he might be assigned to one of the boats, and handle an oar for days along the edge of an inlet very similar to the previous one.

"Chayziz, Bobby, sometimes I think I should rather be one of them Indians than an A.B. in the king's service. Like those two we saw bathing in the sun on that big flat rock last week."

" 'Twas this week."

"Chayziz, it seems like two weeks ago. That's chust what I mean. There's those two sweethearts go set their nets in the mouth of any man's stream and then spend the day how they will, lying in the sun, or carving a walking stick."

"Well, you signed on aboard a hull in His Majesty's fleet, not a savage fishing party, so there's no use to griping."

"Would you please not stand so close, if you are going to be up-breeze of me?"

"You'll be in the king's navy when you can't see as far as that tit-shaped boulder yonder."

"I don't see any tit-shaped boulder."

"You are in this man's navy for your stout back and not your keen eye. Your fate is to be a British sailor, and that's a *fact*."

Upon his pronouncing that last word, the man's entire body dipped and then rose and then settled with a clap on its booted heels.

In truth these men, if they were bored, and they *were* bored, were bored by the ineluctable daily sequence of facts. Whatever the edge of the world was made of, this craft at the nose of the eighteenth century was turning it day by day into facts. Fathoms, leagues, rainfall, names, all facts. The *Discovery* was a fact factory. The charts were covered with numbers and then rolled up and stacked in holes, waiting to be published at home.

Vancouver even wanted to transform the Northwest Passage into a fact.

Every once in a while a couple of men would get tired of facts, and in the dead of night, during a period when the commander and his people were away from the ship, making facts out of another inlet, these men would steal some liquor from stores and proceed to get as far away from facts as they could.

"Chayziz, there's nothing can bring a heart back to a man so fast as a deep draught of the south."

"What south?

"This is some of that stuff the Old Man got off the Spanish poof. They grow it in California. It's not bad for a domestic claret."

"You idiot! It is not a claret, it is a Beaujolais, and furthermore we're going to be in deeper shit than we might have been when we get back to facts; because the Old Man sets a great score upon the stuff the Spaniard gave him. But that's for later. Right now let's have a swig and hear what you have to say for the New World."

"Ah, shit!"

As a matter of fact Vancouver was always most disapproving of liquor offences, whether carried out with domestic or imported products. More sailors were flogged for stealing spirits than for any other misdoing, and punishments were meant to be exemplary. A culprit might expect anywhere from twelve to thirty-six lashes, depending, among other things, upon whether he had got polluted on wine or rum or brandy.

While watching another of those boring punishments, off with the shirt, on with the leather, Menzies found himself standing next to Zack Mudge again. Mudge always winced during the first half-dozen strokes, but then settled down for the count.

"Seven," he said. "Eight. Well? Nine."

Menzies looked at the commander, who as always wore his hat precisely on the centre of his head.

"Not only does he have his own religion," he said at last, "but he has his own way of becoming intoxicated."

"Those two chaps would have done well to have learned it. Twelve," said Mudge.

That evening after dinner Mudge was acting the host as the liqueurs were brought out. Looking at Dr. Menzies without a trace of expression, he gestured toward the bottles on the tray and enquired:

"What's your fancy?"

43

It was time to call it a summer for the first year on the northern coast. October north of the fifty-fifth parallel is not amenable to the exploration of deep fjords. Vancouver set sail for Monterey, looking forward to being once more in the company of Don Juan.

How had the summer gone? Vancouver longed to perform in such a way that his profession would say he could be proud of himself; but part of his pattern of behaviour was a refusal to be proud. The greatest kind of pride. Well, he was not proud of this summer's performance. He had fallen short in all but one of his commissions. The prodigious surveying and map making would have been more than sufficient to justify the expense of raising this expedition. Presumably even the damned Royal Society would appreciate Menzies and his weeds. But Nootka was not yet firmly in British hands. The Northwest Passage was still probably a dozen inlets away. And the only gold and silver he had encountered were upon the table and under the five courses of the meals of which he had partaken at the Spanish commander-in-chief's table.

So Vancouver mentally cursed Juan de Fuca again, and ordered his three ships to be smoked with gunpowder mixed with vinegar, their storerooms washed down with vinegar, and fires ignited between the decks to force old sweaty air out into the sound. Then he had his people bathe, load the vessels with sauerkraut and spruce beer, and the *Discovery*, the *Chatham*, and the *Daedalus* set off for the warm air of California.

As they left Nootka he thought about the last time he had looked at these straight cedars and round rocks with Captain Cook. In his imagination he saw again the reassembled body of his old teacher, and then that corpse mended fully and rose to life again, but this time with the face of Bodega y Quadra. From the decks below rose the satisfying odour of vinegar. The Indian houses at Friendly Cove settled back into obscurity as part of the low land mass. In his imagination Quadra and Cook, both in full naval regalia, leaned over him where he lay, breathing shallowly, in a four-poster bed. It began to rain.

"You had better get in out of this," advised Lieutenant Baker, who was handling the direction of the small fleet this day.

"I hate the rain, Mr. Baker."

"Nobody much likes it, sir, unless he be a farm-owning man."

"I am sometimes afraid in the rain, Mr. Baker. I have had a strange waking dream several times since this summer began."

"That's only your imagination, sir. What do you see in these waking dreams?"

"I see it raining. It is raining hard. I see myself dead in it."

Neither said anything for a while in the embarrassment that seemed to fall on them with the rain. Finally, Baker spoke.

"Well, sir, we will be back in California soon

enough, and there it will not be raining." He waved his arm toward the islands and inlets they were leaving behind. "It's a goodbye to these arms and sounds."

In a few days they arrived near the mouth of the elusive Columbia River. Vancouver ordered Broughton and the *Chatham* to hop over the reef and explore with their boats as deeply as they felt they should up the waterway. Then they were to plant the Flag and claim the river for Britain.

"But the Yankees, sir, have been up the river a year ago. They even named it after their brig."

"I don't give a turd for the Yankees and their claims, mister. They are no nation but a lot of gun merchants and rum salesmen. Perhaps they are past masters at looking for the good thing and the fast dollar. But this is a voyage of exploration and national development, sir; and I am requesting that you place King George's standard in the soil of the Columbia."

Sure, thought Broughton, and we both know that the fur traders will be a good deal happier about the adventure than will be the king, bless his tidal mind.

Vancouver was edgy, and torn between his desire to reach California and his duty, he attended, as ever, without hesitation to his duty and thus his pride. But when he did attain California, he was charming and successful. He made quick friends with the countrified people at the presidio in San Francisco, and relaxed when he saw that this northernmost Spanish bastion was militarily no more than a scenic joke. A tidy little British fleet could overrun it with marines within a day or two. The Spanish soldiers were mainly interested in looking picturesque, though not energetically so. The Indians, unlike the fishermen and boat makers and house builders of the bracing north, were satisfied to sit around in the dirt with colourful though soiled cloth over their knees, and their hands out.

Vancouver was impressed. The soldiers and

sailors of the distant Spanish nation had made it all the way from the tropics to here, with the prime purpose of making Christians of the Indians. The Spanish were as much given to fancy as were the worst of the British command. For hundreds of years the Spanish had been grabbing gold out of the Indians' hands, and giving them wooden crosses in return. Is it any wonder they decided there was nothing to beat sitting around in the dirt?

The Spanish gave the Indians wooden crosses.
The Yankees gave them whiskey.
The English gave them nothing.

44

He got as far south as he was going to go that winter—the National Museum of Costa Rica, which is all about Indians and Spaniards and the great question of religion—before Vancouver did, or before he allowed him to. In this, yet another sequence of rooms filled with artifacts, he found no Strait of Anian, but he was not disappointed. He'd known enough to enter the place expecting to find something for his book by now.

Now, art in San José is not art in Florence. In the museum in San José the old paintings are identified by subject rather than artist. One may expect to harvest little more than a bit of fact here and there. What he found was the answer to a question that had bothered him a few days earlier in another country. What do you call the kind of hat that Captain Vancouver is wearing? You call it a *bicorno*, probably later a *bicuerno*, that is a bicorn. Some eighteenth century naval officers were wearing them in the basement of the Museo Nacional de Costa Rica.

Imagine that.

Vancouver was still going south for the winter, and his lungs were the happier for it. So were his people. At Monterey the crew packed up picnic lunches, and borrowing Spanish horses, rode off into the gentle dry countryside east of that earthly paradise, where the Christian brothers were stamping grapes as if they were gods punishing them. It was a long way from the snows of Kitsilano.

For Vancouver and the other officers it was a sweet Thursday, too. Quadra could be even more generous with his hospitality here because he had greater resources to call upon. The round of parties and dinners began again, but whereas James Broughton had gained five pounds at Friendly Cove, here he gained fifteen. Many of the Spanish functionaries had their families with them, so there were not only feasts and entertainments, but dancing as well.

One evening the wine was flowing copiously, the renowned chef Jacques Pelletier, formerly of Québec, had outdone anything culinary ever tasted on the West Coast, and great shouting and laughter filled the air, sufficient nearly to defeat the efforts of Don Juan's military band. The noise abated for a few moments, then settled into the catchy rhythm of guitars and harp, as four Spanish ladies, in white boots and lace, executed a rattling good fandango. When it was finished Vancouver, as he had done in Hawaii and at Maquinna's village, sought to offer a fair exchange. He therefore sent for the two Hawaiian girls who acted as waitresses and chars on the *Discovery*, to perform a hula dance for his hosts. The four Spanish ladies turned red from their high hairlines to the exposed upper portions of their breasts, raised their fans before their faces, uttered some Spanish phrases marked by dental plosives, and lifting their skirts as they had done in their dance, huffed out of the salon.

"What the . . .?" expostulated Vancouver.

"The ladies appear to have been insulted," said Dr. Menzies. He was not smiling, but he was not frowning, either.

"I believe they were put out to discover that the Island senoritas had prettier legs," commented Joseph Whidbey calmly.

"Damn me, I'm sorry, Don Juan," said Vancouver, looking at Menzies for some reason, with a hatred he had held in abeyance for the last month.

"Do not molest yourself," said Quadra through his interpreter, a young poet from Lima. "Those women do not often get a chance to be scandalized in the thin society we have here. I am certain that I would not be remiss in offering you their thanks on that account."

All this time the Spanish longshoremen were filling the British ships with huge quantities of fresh and salted meat, fresh vegetables, wine and fruits, and typical handicrafts of the region. The scurvy that had begun to insinuate itself among the English during the trip down disappeared, and the men's sexual appetites were once again directed toward women and boys rather than each other and inanimate objects.

It was just the right kind of rest and recreation after an arduous summer of overtime in the northern inlets.

Vancouver said to his host and provisioner, what do I owe you? And Quadra replied, forget it, what are friends for?

"I was hoping that you would let me show you some time when we are not surrounded by a mob of provincial society folk," said Vancouver, who, when he was feeling healthier than usual, almost developed the ability to flirt and otherwise exhibit a sense of humour.

Meanwhile, although they were having a good time ashore, the members of the British crews were still grumbling about their commander. For while he was tremendously cordial with the Spaniards of all conditions, he was strict, cold, aloof, and businesslike with his own officers and men. Ceremonial floggings still went on in this period, and Vancouver even secured the assistance of the Spanish authorities in retrieving for the *Daedalus'* brig several English deserters who had attempted to disguise themselves as Spanish agriculturists in the Salinas Valley.

When a few days later the British vessels sailed for the Sandwich Islands, the carpenter's mate, still feeling insecure after the detention of the ship's carpenter, he who had thought he could get away with telling the captain that he knew more about woodwork than the latter, this carpenter's mate who also felt unable to face life apart from the ex-nun he had been instructing in woodcarving at Pebble Beach, repaired the uppermost portion of the mizzenmast, and then worked his way to the end of the cross spar, and suicided into the sea.

The officers and captains of the *Discovery* and the *Activa* visited one another's ships in their first few days out of Monterey, for the Spaniards were bound for Mexico while the English were on their way to the Sandwich Islands. Just before the unhappy carpenter's mate's body fell past them into the lightly-rippled Pacific off Santa Catalina, this exchange had transpired between Quadra and Vancouver:

"You know, my friend, this coast might not possess the grandeur of the mountains and glaciers of the north, but it has a natural hospitality that feels not unlike a flowered embrace."

"I have never heard you attempt such enheightened language, George. You must indeed have been much impressed."

"It is so attractive, in truth that I am not certain that I shall not press for British control as far south as San Diego."

"Do not press your fancy, my dear friend. You British are fortunate that there is not a Spanish *fuerte* at Cook's River."

"Cook's Inlet."

"Of course, my serious lover of facts."

Vancouver, confident that no one else could see, let his little finger touch Quadra's bottom as they began to stroll around the deck.

"In any event," he summed up, "if California is not fated to be Albion's southwest frontier, I am content that it should remain Spanish. I cannot conceive the misfortune of a California falling to the avaricious hands of the United States."

"That would not be a misfortune," averred the commander-in-chief of the area in question, "it would be a catastrophe."

For days the *Discovery* and the *Activa*, far outpacing their escort vessels, sailed less than a cable's length apart, the Spanish hull with shortened sail to allow Vancouver to keep up. But finally their courses must diverge. Upon the evening of that parting, while the two brilliant sailing ships cut the sea together under a full moon, the Spanish officers sat with their close friends aboard the *Discovery* for a last meal together. The quarterdeck creaked under the weight of the crowded gentlemen in their finest uniforms and polished boots. Wine passed back and forth abundantly, and not a little of it was spirited away to the lads in the rigging. A toast was drunk to London and another to Barcelona, one to peace and one to brotherhood, one to George Vancouver and one to Don Juan Bodega y Quadra. Then a final toast was raised to future meetings, and all at once there was a profound silence.

They tried to rouse the boisterousness again, but it did not work. At midnight, in any case, it was time for the Don and his lieutenants to return to the leaping

Activa. As Quadra stepped from the English ship he turned and saluted its captain. Vancouver wanted to leap forward and before the eyes of all these well-dressed men throw his face upon Quadra's breast. But he returned the salute and gave Puget a crisp command to change course.

As the Peruvian stood upon his ship bent for San Blas, and the Britisher on his ship with a heading westward, the hovering gulls split into two parties to follow the vessels of their calling. George Vancouver heard his birds calling the roll as he looked across the water till all he could see was the silver edge of some clouds driven landward from the southwest.

45

The two Indians were cleaning their fish and spreading them open on the racks leaning over the smoky fire. It was not as simple as the summer method of laying them open on white rocks under the high sun. But in November on the coast there was hardly ever any sun, and when there was there wasn't much.

"Ahkh! Cutting fish open is not as much an interesting occupation as is waiting for the net to fill," said the first Indian.

"Oh, there are worse jobs," said the second Indian. "Be thankful that we are fishermen rather than hunters. Getting the guts out of a salmon is child's play compared with getting the guts out of a bear and taking the hair off. That is a task for a full man of the tribe."

"You will never let me forget that, will you?"

"Oh, it is part of your learning, the making of mistakes and the enduring of jests at your expense. I mean there are fewer and fewer pleasures for us older Indians, and one of them is the opportunity to poke fun at you young fellows."

The first Indian ran the point of his steel knife briskly along a silver belly and flipped the floater and the rest into the creek, all the while leering at his teacher.

"So the *Mamathni* seemed to be ordinary men like ourselves while they were here," he said suggestively.

"Not altogether ordinary, and not like ourselves in many ways. For one thing, they can take their canoes far out to sea. For another they have no women in their races. The two female slaves they carried were brown like ourselves."

"Yes, I wish they had been allowed off the boat. I particularly wanted to touch the taller one, to determine whether she were fact or legend."

"Your wife is a fact, young fellow."

"But as I was saying," continued the first Indian, "they seemed to be men while they were here, but who knows that they were not sent by gods from another land? Or from the Great Spirit Himself? They talked about someone called Blighty, about getting back to him, about how they loved him. Or how about this?Perhaps when they leave our sight they transform themselves back into gods?"

A Yankee named Magee stepped out of the nearby copse with a donkey loaded down with supplies. He held his hand up, palm forward.

"How!" he said, in a deep voice.

The two Indians made their faces look patient.

"What is this 'How'?" asked the first Indian of his companion.

"Search me," said the second Indian. "But we may as well go along with him."

He put his hand up in his best imitation of the skin-covered stranger.

"Aeh, shit!" he said.

"Do you fellows want to buy some whiskey?" asked Magee in his own language, taking a bottle out of a saddlebag.

"No thanks," said the second Indian in his own language.

"Guns?"

"No thanks."

"You want to trade some waterfront property for some mirrors and necklaces?"

"I wouldn't mind having one of those mirrors," said the first Indian to the second Indian.

"Offer him a fish," said the second Indian.

Meanwhile Vancouver's little flotilla of three sails plied westward toward the Islands.

"Are we the *Nina*, the *Pinta*, or the *Santa Maria*?" Menzies asked Vancouver one afternoon. He thought a little quip might warm relations between them a bit. He was mistaken.

"We are not Italians," said Vancouver. "We are British. Juan de Fuca was an Italian. I am sure that I do not have to tell you how I feel about Juan de Fuca."

He enunciated the words as if Menzies might have been a descendant of Juan de Fuca.

"Juan de Fuca was a Greek," said Menzies, wishing he could say something that wouldn't rile the man, and wishing alternatively that he could just bring himself to shut up. Why did he let himself get dragged into one of these scenes?

"He was a citizen of Venice," said Vancouver, never taking his eyes off the chart on the deal table in front of him. "As surely as the putative Greek Tito Melema was a citizen of Florence."

The table had been built by the carpenter's mate the day before he had thrown himself to the sharks. The chart had been provided by the Spanish map agent in Monterey. Upon it was marked a group of islands called Los Mojos. No one but the Spanish had ever run across Los Mojos. They were indicated a few hundred miles east of the Sandwich Islands. People in nautical circles often spoke of Los Mojos, but no one had spied them since the Spanish claim of a century ago. They might have been as chimerical as the Northwest Passage.

"Excuse me, commander, but do you really believe in those Hispanic islands?" asked the doctor. Christ love me, why can't I keep my mouth shut? he thought the while.

"They are there," said Vancouver. But his eyes shifted. His entire physical attitude bespoke his doubt.

Menzies paused to think. I will not say anything. After all I am only a civilian and a botanist. It is no business of mine.

"I have been doing some calculating of my own," he said. "Using those charts, and the Royal Society's new longitude contraption."

He saw Vancouver's lip twitch at the mention of the name.

Vancouver said nothing.

"With the result that I am of the opinion that the Spanish of a hundred years ago miscalculated the sea currents and the winds, and that those are in fact the Sandwich Islands positioned a few hundred miles closer to Peru than they should be."

The lip did not seem to like the mention of that name, either.

Vancouver rolled up the chart and tied it and placed it under his arm. Then he put his hands behind his back. Then he looked Menzies in the face from bloodshot eyes under a straight bicorn hat.

"Mr. Menzies, I am a navigator in the service of His Britannic Majesty."

"Yes you are, and *non pareil* in that capacity."

Vancouver's lip twitched at the sound of the French phrase.

"You are a civilian and a botanist, are you not?" he enquired, polite as a hangman.

"Also a physican."

"You are an accomplished physician. You cured

the Spanish commander-in-chief of a chronic headache, for the which he thanked you with great generosity, and for which I thank you, in the name of better international diplomacy."

Menzies knew there was a but coming.

"But," said the commander. "If Los Mojos are not there, then the Spaniards were visitors to the Sandwich Islands before James Cook landed there, and that would not be an acceptable fact in my view of history. I am during this time having a less than easy experience in establishing the British jurisdiction over Nootka. I do not need a similar entanglement at Hawaii. I assume that you understand my problem. Those Iberian discoveries must be there where this chart fixes them."

Not many days later the *Discovery*, the *Chatham*, and the *Daedalus* sailed through the clear blue waters where Los Mojos were supposed to be, and a few hundred miles later they dropped anchors at Hawaii. Vancouver rubbed noses with the Hawaiian king, delivered the cattle he had brought from California, and gave the Islanders the biggest fireworks display they had ever seen.

A day later he asked the chiefs about last year's killing of some men off the *Daedalus*. The chiefs provided two fishermen, and Vancouver hanged them.

46

A couple of important English politicians were conversing at their club one afternoon in the winter of 1793.

"What are your feelings about the possibility of war?" asked the first Englishman.

"The last thing any Briton desires is to go to war again in Europe and on the Atlantic, but my sources inform me that we are days away from war with Spain," said the second Englishman.

"My sources say that we will be fighting the French before the spring."

"Covington-Grimes insists that the Yankees will invade the American colonies again."

"I really don't see what it is all about," said the first Englishman, looking suspiciously at his sherry.

"Nootka," said his companion.

"What? What is a nutcur?"

"Nootka. A bunch of sheds somewhere on the west coast of British North America."

"Oh yes, indeed, yes. Is that somewhere near Mackinaw?"

"No, no, Mackinaw is somewhere around the Great Lake. You are thinking of Maquinna, and it's not a place. He is the king of those Red Indians out there. They spear whales and the like."

The first Englishman finally took a sip of his sherry. Then he took another sip.

"I say, this Mackiner, are the great nations of the civilized world to go to war over a sunburnt fellow with a basket on his head? I mean, really, Charles. Is there a great deal of gold around Nootker?"

"None at all, according to my sources. There is some talk that Maquinna has enlisted the alliance of our navy because a Spaniard named Martinez put up a huge cross in front of his village."

The first Englishman ordered brandy.

"Aren't all Spanish captains named Martinez, or Hernandez? Wot? Ho ho. And don't they all put up huge crosses, with a Christ hung on them and red paint dripping down his legs?"

The second Englishman put his finger alongside his nose, winked one eye, and motioned his red-faced friend closer. Then he opened a large carpet bag he had been protecting beside his Queen Anne chair. The two bent their unbewigged heads together as Charles opened the bag and lifted from it a sleek pelt, dressed so handsomely that the light from the wall lamps fetched a gleam like Peruvian silver from the million fine hairs.

"Good Lord! Excuse me," said the first Englishman spilling strong drink on his friend's boot. "That is the richest, most splendid fur these old eyes have ever had the privilege to see. I need not tell you that they have seen a great many upon the back of a lady whose name shall remain unspoken, wot?"

"It is called a Pacific sea otter," said Charles, rippling it like silver velvet in the glow. "They frolic only in the waters off the coast in question. My sources tell me that the celestials in Canton will barter a lap-full of ivory carvings for a middling-good example of this."

He put the pelt again into its cradle, and leaning back in his chair, made a steeple of his fingers and smiled like the pasha he had until recently been.

"Covington-Grimes is an ass, but he may have fallen upon wisdom concerning the noted business sense of the Yankees. So this skin has brought the kingdoms of the civilized world to another armament?" mused the first Englishman.

"Not to mention the tsardoms, and the republics."

The moist and red-rimmed eyes of the first Englishman took on a sparkle of sorts.

"Now I understand a little more about the Admiralty's relations with the Pacific barbarians," he said. "One will keep one's eyes peeled for news of this Nootker royalty, and his continuing Maquinnations, don't you think?"

The second Englishman gathered his bag and his rotund figure together, and prepared to rise.

"I must be off now, old nut. My niece is taking me around to some woebegone printer's shop to look at a portmanteau of engravings. Some new discovery of hers, a lunatic called Black, or Block, dash it, I cannot recall. Apparently makes pictures of angels falling head-forward from the sky. I don't know how I let myself in for such foolishness."

"Why don't you place the sea otter over her shoulders and tell her that she is angel enow?"

"Wish I could, old bean. But you know the young ladies today. Always taking a fancy for whatever novelty they can surprise in less pleasant-smelling parts of the town."

"Well," said the first Englishman. "I thank the Anglican God that I am too old for nieces, too practical for art, and too grey for war."

Whereupon he signalled to the captain for more sherry.

47

Each of us is a man turning to say farewell. It is a condition we must enter whether we will or no.

Vancouver began his career and all his voyages with the feeling that he was going out there to say hello. But somewhere in the last year he had begun to notice the turnings and the goodbyes, and now it was goodbye to most of himself, goodbye to the years of himself left here and there on islands scattered in his wake. Goodbye the body's capacity for love.

He had been a great success on the Sandwich Islands again, settling their political squabbles and putting an end to the civil war that had laid waste to farmlands he had done so much to promote. Now he had supplied them again with livestock, brought the wisdom of King George to Chiefs Titeere and Tamaahmoah, and administered their peace.

But his notorious aloofness was becoming colder and colder. Ever since he had hanged the two fishermen, his own men turned their eyes away when he approached. He had become more strict than ever before about visitors, and men were heard to grumble between the decks.

Peter Puget wrote in his diary: "Since Captain Vancouver's Intentions, however trifling in themselves are always under a seal we can form no judgement of the present plan."

Puget felt the same way about commas that he felt about natives. The fewer the better.

The men became really deeply angry that winter when Vancouver restricted them for most of the time to their shipboard quarters, while he himself was usually ashore eating and talking and trading objects with chiefs and kings of Hawaii and Mauii.

"Sir?" uttered Joseph Whidbey, a friend of the men, one day as Vancouver was stepping into the launch.

"Don't even ask it," said the captain.

Women did run free aboard the ships, and offered authentic comforts to men who had finished an exhausting season of work and looked forward to nothing beyond another. But they would have liked to go and lie upon one of those white beaches, give their bodies to the surf, go upstream and stand under a cool waterfall, return to the green-blue ocean and order a coconut full of heady drink. It was some solace but not enough that they could look forward every night to a Hawaiian massage administered by a bare-breasted heathen woman.

Nor was it enough solace that the Old Man had to spend every second day flat on his back in his sick bed.

He was probably just lying there thinking dirty thoughts about his Spanish pal, anyway. But his surgeon knew better; he knew that Vancouver had gone to war with his body now, a war that he would have to lose before a proper truce could be signed. Menzies tended him and advised him, but he seethed with anger, or more properly disgust, about the displacement of feelings that had the usually fair and sane commander applying bitter restraint upon those he formerly liked to call his people.

Was George Vancouver a crazy man? The

thought entered quickly and unbidden, and Menzies frowned as it remained behind his wrinkled forehead. Vancouver crazy? Menzies thought about the deserters at Monterey.

The first deserter from the *Discovery* had secreted himself inside the Carmelite monastery at Monterey. He was a desperate man. It was likely that if he should succeed in his effort to avoid revisiting the north coast, he would never see Britian again, nor live in a society in which the language of the street was his own. He was twenty years old and not an orphan, but he chose this moment to escape Captain George Vancouver. He knew that Vancouver made a point of respecting Spanish customs, and he knew that asylum in a church building was a Spanish custom. What he did not count on was the influence that Vancouver had with Quadra, who was commander of the Carmelites as well as everyone else in a country so close to the edge of the world during a time when the friendship between two men, and how it was conducted, might keep a continent halfway around the world away from war, and twenty-year-old boys alive a little longer.

The upshot was that through his amity with Quadra, Vancouver had the boy dragged from the chapel, clapped in irons, given seventy-two lashes in front of the whole company, clapped in irons in the brig once more, and a week later again given seventy-two lashes in front of the whole ship's company.

"May I attend to the boy?" asked Menzies.

"The law says that you may and indeed should look at, the *man*, sir," replied the commander.

Vancouver began coughing, and his will fought his body, not permitting it to bend. This was the day after Quadra had waved over to the English ship for the last time.

There had been other plans to jump ship at Monterey, and one crewman, the armorer off the *Chatham*, had succeeded. He had disappeared from sight. In all probability he would somewhere in a warm valley begin a family that carried an English surname but spoke Spanish for a few generations before it learned to speak English again. Vancouver enlisted Quadra's aid once more, but neither Vancouver's marines nor Quadra's fusiliers could track the fugitive. To show the extent of his hospitality and his honest desire for peace, Quadra selected an armorer from his own contingent and compelled the poor Iberian to sail aboard the *Chatham* in recompense for the strayed Briton.

Menzies suspected that such occurrences were perhaps creative but not untoward in the world of the overseas navy. But he did not love for it the coughing and sweating man under his care. When the ship anchored off Mauii, he went for an extensive botanical excursion to the interior, half hoping that the tyrant would not survive his absence, and might share his mentor's fate among these tropical isles.

But upon his return he found the man still on his feet more days than half, his lungs improving in condition even while his emotional attitude, toward the natives as well as toward his own men, exhibited some bizarre turns. Menzies was put in mind of their argument about the Islanders' slash fires last year. He wondered how to imagine the fancies taking root in the man's mind now, in regard to the people's behaviour.

There were times when he seemed still the man that Cook had trained: fair and discerning, open to the manners of the exotic. But other times he seemed given to an unexaminable fear. More than once Menzies observed him to spin suddenly around, as if to catch an unwelcome observer below decks or on the promenade. Once the patient caught the physician noticing such an occurrence.

"What are you looking at?" snapped Vancouver.

"Only what the scientist is prepared for and satisfied with. The data."

"I am not data, leech."

"The word means that which is given. Yet the gift does not become property," said Menzies.

Vancouver often made gifts and he often received them, usually for political reasons, such was his talent. But one day at Mauii he showed another attitude toward property, one that transpired from time to time, as in the cases of ship's liquor and cutlery.

This time the island's king was enjoying a visit on the *Discovery* when a fuss was raised about a piece of blue ribbon. The Englishmen made a practice of giving lengths of ribbon to the women from time to time, convincing them that they were of considerable value. By means of such ploys, a length of ribbon did take on considerable value in this society, much in the way gold and silver do elsewhere. Blue ribbon was worth twice as much as red ribbon, etcetera.

But on this occasion, someone with a brown skin had lifted the blue ribbon from a young woman who had earned it from an able seaman. Waxing all the while louder and more importunate, the young woman in question shouted aloud her loss to everyone she could find, the noise growing closer and closer to the captain's quarters, where he was talking politics with the king.

The girl burst into the chamber, weeping, waving her hands, stamping her bare feet, until Vancouver, having spilled his spruce beer while rising, enquired of the ship's master, who followed the distraught creature into the room, what had transpired, and hearing the outline of the case, began to display some animation himself.

He grasped his sword from its position on the bulkhead and waved it over his head.

"I shall find the slave who purloined this damned cloth, and when I do he will wish that he had remained by his mother's knee, pounding *poi*!" he shouted.

The girl shrieked as the sword scraped across a mirror, spilling shards onto a chair. The king of Mauii pulled his old thin body through a window and dropped into the sea, where he swam until an escort *proa* picked him up. Mr. Whidbey backed out of the room and walked quickly and quietly away, determined never to mention the scene to anyone.

He *is* crazy, thought Menzies.

These people are all crazy, thought Vancouver. He turned and said farewell to something but he was too worn out to imagine what it was.

48

Farewell, farewell. On the way to the north coast they stopped at Monterey, which Vancouver approached with longing and fear in his innards. Sure enough, when they got there there was no sign of Bodega y Quadra. Vancouver saluted the acting governor, José Joaquin de Arrillaja, and enquired about his old friend.

"I am not authorized to give that information to the English," the acting governor replied icily.

"What *are* you authorized to give to the English?" asked Vancouver, trying not to sound testy. His diplomacy, along with his other mental powers, had slipped a little of late.

"You may anchor here for a period of two days the while you are purchasing fuel and water and the like," said the icy one. "Then you will be eager, I am sure, to proceed northward."

As often happened, Menzies dropped protocol, enquiring: "Last autumn I began a horticultural project in these parts. I should like to visit the sites I have been studying."

"You will, I am sure, find many plants and trees farther north. In the meantime I feel bound to caution you to remain on board your ships save on the occasions when I invite some of the officers for dinner or the like."

Vancouver's unprepossessing neck was stiff. His eyes stared from their softened sockets. He clapped his bicorn squarely on his head.

"This treatment will not sit well in Britain and Europe, sir," he said.

"Europe is at arms. Louis XVI has lost his head to the new crowd. As for Britain, she has fully sufficient problems in dealing with republicans on her own soil and Dutch ships in her channel. You will be doing excellent well to get to Cook's River as fast as you can sail. Good day, sir."

Vancouver sank onto a chair.

"Cook's Inlet," he murmured.

Menzies took a look at him and ordered him to bed immediately. For a change the commander went without an argument. He lay in his bed and quietly disputed the fever that desired to enter at his eyes and rummage around in his brain. Where was Quadra? Had he been deposed for his generosity to the English? Was he at Nootka again, or in the Bering Sea, warring with Russians? No, the Spanish did not like to venture that far north. But Quadra had done so, alone that time. But he was not that reckless young man any more. Neither was George Vancouver.

He remained confined to his quarters until the expedition attained Nootka. There he was met by another shock. Upon an island in the bay stood a new Spanish fort, with nine guns trained on the British ships.

"This is an outrage," whispered Vancouver, buckling his sword belt.

"I wonder whether they call it Friendly Cove Fort," mused Whidbey.

Here too, they were allowed to drop anchors while they replaced depleted supplies. Quadra, of course, was not at Nootka. But the Yankees were. They crawled all over the trading post and the military grounds like flies on a pastry, trading in liquor and arms, gathering in furs and gold coin, and looking for an opportunity to scoop up some real estate. The new Spanish commander was an army man, General José Alva. Vancouver could never warm to anyone named Joseph, whether he represented the Royal Society or the Spanish crown. Even with his ship's master he was only upon terms polite.

"What news do you have of Don Juan Bodega y Quadra?" asked the man who had named this whole island.

"I am not at liberty to divulge that information at this time," said the Spaniard in a manner as stiff as only a Spanish general officer could achieve.

"There will be no island nor mountain nor inlet named Alva in these parts," vowed Captain Vancouver after he had left the new administration offices.

"I wonder where Commander Quadra is?" said Lieutenant Baker.

"We will not pursue such idle fancies," snapped Vancouver, and Baker exchanged glances with his fellow officers.

Magee the bootlegger approached the group as they were preparing to board their launch. He had five donkeys loaded down with bags and boxes.

"Could I interest you gentlemen in some sure as shootin' Jamaickey rum?" he asked, looking at them out of the sides of his eyes.

"See the officer of stores," said Mr. Baker. "But listen carefully, Yankee. See that you do not suggest to him an exorbitant price. He has a very slow sense of humour, and likes to push bad-smelling Yankee traders into the drink."

"How about some interestin' Indian trinkets?" said Magee, opening a box and extracting several leathern sacks depending from cords made of beaded hide. These were medicine bundles, and no Red Man would in any circumstance trade them for whiskey or ammunition.

"Where did you come by these?" asked Menzies.

"Why, they are trophies, Mister. I bagged the specimens which was wearin' them, and left the meat for the poor starvin' coyotes."

"You shot those people for their apparel?" asked Baker.

"Surely, son. What do *you* do with the wild heathens? Go dancing and dining with 'em?"

"Get away from us, fellow, or we will instruct you in a dance you never saw unless you be from the hell you are clearly destined for," said Peter Puget. That was a surprise.

As the launch crossed the slightly choppy water between the pier and the *Discovery*, Vancouver sat in the stern, a blanket over his shoulders and a look on his face that signalled a soul concentrating in order to hide a body's pain. Each of the several gentlemen who saw his face foresaw a summer during which that pain would be distributed among all the hands aboard the *Discovery* and the *Chatham*.

49

After wandering around Limón during a January afternoon, perspiring through a Vancouver City College T-shirt, he understood even less those Spanish marines and cavalry and foot soldiers he had seen in numerous murals over the years, stamping and crashing through whatever plant growth used to be here before the bananas and coconuts, in full armour, that triangulated Spanish armour, from toe to helmet, plus whatever they wore underneath. He supposed that the tropic sun reflected off the metal, but those ordinary everyday conquistadores had to do their clanking and grunting when the sun was directly overhead, too.

But what had they been looking for? The fountain of eternal youth, which would have been taken over immediately by the nobility. Gold and silver and precious stones. Converts to the Lord.

Limón is a peculiar place. The European-looking people speak Spanish, and the African-looking people speak English. There are hardly any Indians, but the ones who plied boats about this coast a few hundred years ago had a language that depended a lot on dreams. No one ever wrote it down.

He was straining for a comparison, or even a connection, with Nootka. It is winter up there right now, he thought, on the other coast, kitty-corner from here. He always seemed to be at some geographical or marine end of something.

If he could just bring Captain Vancouver to being as alone as he had made himself.

It was back to the foot-by-foot work on the serrate coast, but this summer they were farther north, among less friendly natives, and under almost daily rainfall.

Now, no matter how Captain Vancouver felt about the Spanish, the French, Menzies, the Islanders, the Yankees, and all the other enemies he had recently acquired in his mind, his chiefest foe of all was the wet weather.

"Do you really think the rain can be that dangerous to him?" asked Puget of Menzies one afternoon, as they watched the captain standing with one hand on the rail, something he had never permitted himself to do in his best days. He was overseeing the fitting of the boats, and doing his best, his throat jumping, to stifle a cough.

"The rain?" said Menzies after his customary rhetorical pause. "Sometimes I see him dead in it."

Vancouver did not go out in that rain very often. He was seldom seen in the boats now, as the dull and repetitious work was carried on chiefly under the direction of Mr. Johnstone, his best surveyor, and the charts were drawn by the talented and usefully unimaginative Lieutenant Baker.

The men faced the certainty of harder and harder labour in colder and colder conditions with Protestant quietness. Vancouver applied three innovations: he worked them longer hours so that they might take advantage of the later sunlight and finish the edge of the continent in but two more summers; he had canvas canopies fashioned for the boats, plus improved waterproof tents and bags for the campsites; and he instituted the practice of providing two hot meals a day. When seamen Carter died rolling on the ground after eating some mussels, he had an officer assigned daily to record what the men were eating.

But he got excited and insisted upon attending the expedition when they came to Los Reyes River, marked on Camaaño's 1792 map as the passage indicated by de Fonté. Perhaps he felt that being this far north he would have no subsequent chance to sail his flag to Hudson's Bay. So he set out in the boats, along with Menzies, Puget, Sykes, the miscreant Pitt, and Swaine. In three weeks they had measured their way to the mouth of the waterway circling Revilla Gigedo Island, and landed there to make camp and rest, to put away the diagrams already limned, and oil the ropes, caulk the leaks, repair the loose oarlocks, for the plunge into the heart of the continent.

"Not a chance," said Menzies.

"I always leave room for a little of maybe," said Jonathan Sykes goodnaturedly.

"I say not a chance forcefully as I can manage, to balance his silly optimism."

"You think he believes it, Menzies?"

"I think he is the greatest pessimist of us all. That is why he is the premier sea surveyor of our age," said Menzies, and Sykes believed that he followed the path of the surgeon's discourse.

They looked up to espy several canoes approaching in the late evening light. Vancouver signalled for one man to prepare whatever gifts they could manage, and some others to situate themselves in advantageous positions with their weapons.

The six canoes kept coming until the people aboard them could lay their hands on English property. The brash thieving party was seen to be led by an old woman with the braided grey hair that looks so good on women with deep-tanned skin. The Indians, without any address to the white men, started to pick things up, not even bothering to smile at the owners. It was as if they had received a lading manifest to come and retrieve this stuff.

"God curse you, that is enough!" shouted Vancouver frightening his own men by the force of his unwonted fire. He brandished a musket. The Indians dropped the stuff and let their canoes drift back a piece. Then they were seen to have nearly surrounded the Englishmen, all but a few holding upraised spears.

"I have had my belly filled with uncivilized people who take, take, take," said Captain Vancouver.

"This is a queer pass," commented Menzies in an aside to Sykes. "It frightens me for what it bodes in that man's brain, but you know, I have to admit that I rather like it."

The canoes were drifting almost imperceptibly closer to the stores. When Vancouver perceived the fact, he ordered a volley of pistol and musket. The officers and men filled the air with smoke and sound, the Indians threw their spears, grabbed what they could, and scattered into the fading twilight.

When it was all over there were two wounded sailors, and eight dead Indians, some of them probably sons of the gang's leader. Vancouver had slumped onto the wobbly stool made for him by the late carpenter's mate. The last dying Indian was brought to him and dumped at his feet. Menzies looked him over and signalled that he was through.

"What was this all about?" Vancouver asked the teeth-gritting man in Tlingit.

"You Russians!" grated the man.

"No, we are not Russians."

"You Yankees, you Russians and you Yankees! You make us go to war with our sacred enemies, the Tsetsaut, and then you take all our sea otter furs and give us muskets that do not function. You rabbit fuckers!"

Whereupon saying, he died.

"I am really getting sick of all this," said Vancouver. He ordered the eight bodies to be carried to the edge of a defile and dumped over.

"We will call this place Escape Point," he instructed his scrivener.

Not very original, thought Menzies.

50

Sometimes I picture myself fixing a great explosive store amidships and just blasting her to the bottom of the deep sea off the bench, said Captain Vancouver to himself, or more properly to Don Juan Bodega y Quadra. That was the absent person to whom he addressed his interior monologue these days. It used to be Captain Cook, but Vancouver found it preferable to address his thoughts to an older man who, while he was not present, neither was he dead.

In fact H.M.S. *Discovery* was on a fair way to dropping anyway, from the slow explosion of old age. When the men bruised their backs rowing the old tub from point to point, all her junctures complained of the pull. Ropes broke and cables snapped, and three anchors were lost to the scant sea bottom.

One afternoon the tired lady sat at the front of a fresh gale and led the healthy *Chatham* right into the strait inside Banks Island. Immediately they found themselves surrounded by small rock outcroppings and tangles of water that promised reefs and hidden ledges. The wind became even more insistent, banging water off those rocks, snapping lines against the masts, while the mist began to turn to fog. It was the wrong place to be, especially with a ship that might crumble under a hammer blow.

Maybe it would simplify matters if I just put on all the sail I can find and run the rocks, thought Vancouver.

Yes, surely, that would get you your Northwest Passage, that is certain, Quadra said in return. Seemed to say.

It got more difficult to see as the sun commenced to fall behind the thick mist. Vancouver could make out the faces of three of his officers. They all looked at him and listened. All three of them were thinking at him as hard as they could: *Turn back. Get us out of this.*

He held on. The rocks became thicker, and the submerged ones seemed from the appearance of the dashing, snarling water, to cross the whole channel. There was no question of anchoring: the wind would swing the ships until their sides were smashed to lumber. Yet the light was disappearing. In another hour they would have to take their chances with questionable anchors and rotting lines tied to poorly-rooted trees in a wind that would almost certainly increase and spin them to their plunge.

They were at the upper left corner of the world, utterly alone, and before the night was over they would become one of the many mysteries of the sea.

"I see a ship, sir," said Whidbey.

Nothing, at that moment, could have enraged Vancouver more.

"Keep quiet, Master Whidbey!" he yelled, into the wind.

As if these rock-strewn straits are always filled with seagoing traffic at this time of night here in the extremity.

"I'm sorry, sir, I'm certain I see a ship, coming this way."

You *want* to see a ship, man. *I* want to see a ship, too. I want to see the Angels of the Lord descend and carry my ships to a tranquil beach. No, I want them to lay us down at the mouth of Anian's Strait. I want new rope and fresh planking to make the voyage with, and a hot cup of tea with the British governer at Hudson's Bay.

"Sir," shouted Mr. Baker, "there *is* a ship approaching."

It was a whaler, and if it could be believed, a British whaler, lifting on the swells and plunging over the swells. The *Discovery* lined up behind her, and rode as safely between clapping towers of white water. In an hour it was dark, but there were five British ships at quiet anchor in a sheltered cove. Captain Brown of the *Butterworth* saluted the navy with seven guns, and Vancouver replied with five, which was according to the rules. He would have liked to fire nine. Thus, when Captain Brown and his men came over to visit they were filled with wonderment upon receiving excellent Spanish brandy.

The civilian officers were interested to hear of Vancouver's work, and they were especially animated upon hearing of his recent run-in with the old Indian woman and her gang.

"Yes, we have met her," said Captain Brown. "She wanted to buy some muskets from us, but as you know, our charter forbids our trading weapons to the aborigines."

He smiled as he tasted his brandy.

"They were hollering something about the Russians and the Yankees," said Menzies.

"Well, you know we are used to the Yankee, who would sell a bomb to the enemy of his brother. But the Russian, he is a puzzling chap. There are those who are inciting the tribes against each other, it is true, just so that they might find a market for the surplus of second-rate muskets. But I have met some good Russians, too."

"So have we," said Vancouver. He could not believe how quickly he had become bored after resigning himself and all his people to painful death.

"The, uh, aroma . . ." began Mr. Brown.

"The Russian fur trader," said Vancouver, knocking the bottom of his cup upon the board, "offers a most intolerable stench, the worst excepting the skunk, that I have ever had the inconvenience of experiencing."

"What of the British whaler?" asked Mr. Brown, looking mischievously over the brim of his drink.

"You do not possess any bouquet at all," said Vancouver. "You are a barely substantial angel who comes to dying sailors out of the mist."

"I hope," said Mr. Brown, "that you will encounter more pleasant surprises on your way northward. A little pace north of here we were standing off the opening of a very large waterway, and chanced to meet some canoes coming from the interior. On conversing with these paddlers we heard them claim that they had proceeded eastward a month to barter with an Indian people completely alien to them."

"I do not believe it," said Vancouver.

51

The river and the riverbank were filled and covered with gold. Partly because they were tired of dried Spanish beef, and partly for the sport of it, Vancouver's men walked among the spawning humpback salmon, spearing hundreds of them. Seaman Delsing closed his eyes and thrust his spear downward. Miraculously he did not hit one of the frantic dying fish, but instead pierced his boot and nearly removed his third toe. Dr. Menzies patched him up and told him he was a fool.

"I *am* a fool," said the sailor. "I am a poet, too."

"Oh well, I am a god from the sun," muttered Menzies, tearing the bandages and tying the ends.

"I am preparing a long poem about our search for El Dorado and the Strait of Anian," said the youth.

"I am preparing a long poem, too," said Menzies, putting away his things. "It uses as its central metaphor the flora of newly discovered lands."

"An interesting fancy," said the bandaged sailor.

"Get out of my sight, you idiot," said Menzies.

God, sometimes he wished the expedition was

ended and the creaky old *Discovery* rocking on the small waves at Plymouth.

It turned out that the gold salmon were poor eating. Menzies took a few bites, turned the fish over and over on his plate, and retired to his greenhouse to make notes. It was as he had predicted to himself alone this time: the masculine humpback fought his way up the fierce river to his goal, achieved what he had been preparing for all this time in the open sea, and perished.

At this moment Captain Vancouver was alone on the afterdeck, thinking about that which he had not told anyone, except Quadra.

During their close encounter with the old woman and her gang of toughs, he had seen one demon wearing a painted wolf mask point a stained musket straight at his chest. Remembering this, he coughed, and felt a fist of pain in the middle of his breast. He had heard the hammer fall and an imaginary ball went through him, emerging from the middle of his back. So he was personally satisfied that the Russians or Yankees had been passing off bum firearms to those louts. But now he remembered that when the Indian pointed the barrel at his chest he could have moved, he could even have dived into the water. But he had not dodged. If anything, he had faced the savage a trifle more squarely. Perhaps his dignity was involved. Perhaps that was it.

But now he was becoming more nervous every day about his health, and wondered seriously whether he would return to London either through the Northwest Passage or around the Horn. Or would the bilious colic see to it that like most of his friends, or rather peers, he would remain somewhere in the world little known. If this happened he was going to see to it that from the Tropic of Cancer to the Arctic Circle, other sea captains would be desirous of using his charts to find the place where the disposition of his remains might be made.

"Damn," said one of his lieutenants to another one day. "I can understand his not wanting to depend upon the Spanish maps."

"They are very good for what they do, but they hop across the mouths of the inlets."

"That's what I mean," said the first lieutenant. "The men have just come aboard after twenty-three days, during which time they rowed seven hundred miles. Now we are sixty miles farther up the coast."

"Well, you know he was in error about the Columbia River," said the second Lieutenant. "Now he is resolved not to miss a slight turn in a piss creek."

"As I say, I can understand his remeasuring the foreign maps, but he does not even trust the word of Cook's maps, and he was with Cook."

"Maybe that is why."

"Don't be facetious. I think that the Old Man wants to be perfect because no one likes him, and he will be entitled to say to anyone, 'I care not whether I have your liking, because being perfect I can do well enough without it.' "

"Well, aren't you the imaginative one? How did you get so clever? I thought you rose from master's mate just as I did myself," drawled the second lieutenant.

"Ah yes, but all the time we were on Hawaii you were wasting your charms on that chief's son . . ."

"Daughter."

"Chief's daughter, while I was loitering about the hut of Kamekama's magic man. He told me many useful things that will stand me in good stead when I have my own command. Among them is the ability to read men's characters by the movements of all parts of their bodies. That is how I know that Vancouver aches for perfection out of loneliness. He is unbending."

"I have heard it said that he did bend for a certain Spanish officer."

"Your rude jests shelter an unadventurous mind."

"Did you learn to read the man's future, too?" asked the second lieutenant. "For that is what men ever seek to learn from soothsayers."

"The art of which I speak is something more remindful of science than of fortune telling," said the first lieutenant.

"So what does grass-hut science have to say about our commander's future?"

The first lieutenant looked suddenly hard into the other's eyes, as if what he was seeing for the first time he was seeing there.

"I think that I am closer to that command than I had thought possible," he said in a voice touched by pleasure, then made quickly brusque.

53

The farther north they went, the fewer the inlets left into which one might carry a hopeful heart, the farther these tired Englishmen were from the fruit trees, the thicker the grease grew upon the knicked and darkening tables. Dr. Menzies had proven an old suspicion of his, that scurvy was indeed discouraged by the juice of citrus fruit and by Coevorden's foul-tasting sauerkraut, but more important now that the limes were all gone, it was promoted by grease.

"If you will have the cook make soap, we will remove most of the grease, and retard the scurvy," he said at the table one evening.

All the officers were spooning grey stew into their mouths, and staring at the table an inch in front of their bowls.

"The men are consuming grease apurpose, mister, in order to keep warm during long days in the cold rain," said Mr. Johnstone, without looking up.

"Frobisher learned grease eating from the Arctic natives, but his crews died or languished from the greatest scurvy seen upon an English expedition," said Menzies.

"Captain Frobisher made the most courageous voyage ever essayed," said Vancouver with anger. "While the pie eaters in the Linnean Society were discussing the feasibility of carrying geese upon Arctic expeditions as a ready source of down filling."

Peter Puget drank down a short ration of beer, and raised his head in such a way that he commanded what little attention the weary company had to offer.

"Dr. Menzies. If you would keep us as free from the accumulation of grease as you make yourself so occupied to do, I would suggest that you forbid visits to His Majesty's sailing ships by your dark-complected heathen friends."

Vancouver snorted.

But in fact, the farther north they travelled the more intransigent did the Indian tribes become. In Lynn Canal, named with a mockery of sentiment for the commander's birthplace, Whidbey's party had been nearly done away with by what seemed an entire community of natives, men and women.

The canoes filled with warriors and, propelled by the paddles of old women with loose grey hair, appeared by threes and fours from up the waterway. In several of them could be seen their chiefs, standing and gesticulating, holding wooden boxes and wearing wooden helmets straight on their heads.

Now there were at least two hundred savages, many carrying muskets or blunderbusses of various design, the rest holding spears with jagged barbs. In the longest dugout of all stood a skinny old chief, covered from the shoulders down with goat hair that had been dyed brilliant colours, long coloured streamers hanging from beneath his wooden helmet.

"What does this mean?" asked Whidbey of his Nootka guide.

"They are not our friends," said the guide.

The unfriendly Indians were shouting and waving their weapons.

"What do they want?" asked Whidbey.

"They would enjoy having our boats and everything that is in them, Joseph."

"Then they will have to take them when we are all of us dead," said Whidbey, his chins raised in British pride.

"God, I hate this," a sailor said.

The skinny old chief had brought his canoe alongside the much smaller English boat. He stepped across the gunwhale and picked up a length of chain. Whidbey stepped on the chain and pushed the old fellow back into his canoe, where he fell noisily and proceeded to scream. Whidbey wiped the greasy dye from his hands onto his trouser leg.

He ordered his boats to make for the middle of the canal, to hold their fire ready but not to discharge their muskets and pistols until he gave the order.

The canoes manoeuvered until they had surrounded the British boats. The sunlight poured down from between two clouds.

"Tell them that we are gods, and that we cannot be pierced by balls or blades," Whidbey instructed his guide.

When the man had hollered this message, the men in the canoes laughed and shouted derisively. Then a younger chief picked up a bark megaphone and shouted a long gutteral message back to the white men. It was punctuated by supportive expletives from the warriors and high pitched curses from the hags.

The sailors looked to their master. Whidbey raised his thick eyebrows toward the guide. The guide shook his head.

"Aeh, shit!" he said. "They say that you should go and be gods in your own land. They say you are not permitted to step your sacred *Mamathni* feet upon their mother."

"We don't care about their old women. Will you tell them that we only want to measure the depth of their water and the length of their waterfront?"

"By their mother they mean the continent," said the guide.

In such fashion did Lynn Canal become the first inlet north of Baja California not to be surveyed exactly to its head. Thus was the dream of perfection to disappear behind an ice-laden cloud.

54

He was mainly perplexed that two men like Vancouver and Menzies, who so much resembled one another in energy, professional devotedness, and pride, should be at such odds during their voyage. But then he remembered that a beautiful girl likes to pal around with a plain girl. Great actresses make their most enduring marriages with businessmen whose names are well known only in the business world. So Vancouver might have been able to put up with the little round Scotchman, he decided, if the latter had been a passable surgeon or botanist, and a complete dunce when it came to observing, measuring, and keeping himself perpendicular on the planet.

But in the spring of 1794, the little doctor packed some barometers and other gadgets and climbed Moana Loa, whose altitude, he pronounced, was 13,634 feet above mean sea level. One hundred and eighty-four years later it was 13,680 feet, and there are two possibilities: Menzies' calculations were forty-six feet, or 0.033625 percent off the mark; or the mountain has grown by 0.033625 percent in just under two hundred years. His decision, or his guess, was that the fact lay somewhere in between. In any case, an eighteenth-century surveyor would probably have considered 99.66375 percent accuracy close enough to perfection, especially for an amateur. It was, he thought, better than the pure soap that some people settled for and others boasted of. But then he had heard recently what Vancouver's later opinion of soap was, or at least his attitude toward Menzies' opinion of soap as opposed to grease.

And this: he was more than beginning to concur with Menzies' apprehension or perhaps diagnosis of the commander's mental condition.

When the ships limped into Nootka, scarred by ice, creaking and groaning in all their joints, and manned by weak, stinking crews, Vancouver nevertheless employed the last of the powder in saluting the Spanish flag, and received the answering salvo. He managed to dress himself in shining brass and affected a modicum of hope along with surprising dignity, though his once beefy figure was near to collapsing inside the cloth.

General Alva told him that there was yet no final word from Madrid concerning the political disposition of the trading station. There were Yankee rum purveyors all over the post, and even a brace of Yankee gunships at rest just outside the harbour.

Over a hospitable but by no means elegant dinner, Vancouver got the conversation around to the subject of his principal curiosity.

"While most grateful for your welcome after the ice and high seas of New Norfolk," he said, "I was rather hoping to find your naval commander-in-chief here."

"He has not been here for well past a year," said the general.

"Perhaps I shall find him at Monterey."

Alva placed into his mouth a large piece of roasted chicken.

"Don Juan Bodega y Quadra died in Mejico last year," said a *subalterno*, following a short silence.

I'm happier than you can imagine that you could come over tonight.

That night Vancouver took early to his bed, and remained there during the days that the British ships were outfitted. He remained there as Baker managed the journey southward, and when he finally showed himself upon the deck they were already south of the Columbia, making for the Spanish coast.

By the time they met the *Daedalus* he had regained the control of their course though not of his own. Every second day he ordered a sailor flogged, and then halted the proceedings after a few lashes. The appearance of the supply ship and the hope that Pitt and Clarke were bringing definitive news from Australia nearly caused him to smile.

But the *Daedalus* had no news. The Admiralty was preoccupied with its military campaigns on the other ocean, and seemed to have forgotten the crown's little commission in the fabulous North Pacific.

Vancouver laughed in a high-pitched voice. His lieutenants looked at one another in alarm as he doubled over the taffrail, alternately laughing and choking on the foul liquid rising from his lungs.

"Perhaps we should bring them a Northwest Passage filled with the awfullest monsters of the deep," he shouted.

"Mayhap they were consigning us to a vaporous dream from the first," offered Joseph Whidbey, hoping to establish that Vancouver was finding an outlet from stress in humorous fancy. "That is why they despatched us upon All Fool's Day."

Vancouver stood himself up straight and fixed his bicorn squarely on his head.

"Mr. Whidbey," he said, "we shall return to Britian, and we shall return not as fools but as sailors who have worked harder than any other men in the history of the sea. Do you know what we have worked so hard for? To bring detailed and correct information from around the world to lay before powerful men who live on speculations and require miracles."

"Yes sir," said the master, who had been responsible for demanding that hard work of his young men.

"We will be proud of our work, mister," said the captain. "As proud as any pirate who ever managed to sink the king's foe."

55

Despite everything, the Old Man was pleased to have disproved the claims of Juan de Fuca and de Fonté, partly because they were not English, but mainly because they had been men who did not even prize the vain attempt at the perfect. They were not scientists and they were not artists; they were men who dreamed of themselves.

Vancouver thought: could I be mad?

He looked up at the tern resting on the topmost stay, tail into the wind, and asked: am I mad?

It is a question that any man must ask after he has spent himself upon a principle he could have learnt only from the world, only to find that the world does not agree with him. It may assent, but it does not agree with him.

> How changed the scene! Overhead a sweet blue haze distilling sunlight in drops. And flung abroad over the visible creation was the sun-spangled, azure, rustling robe of the ocean, ermined with wave crests, all else infinitely blue. Such a cadence

of musical sounds! Waves chasing each other and sporting and frothing in frolicsome foam, painted fish rippling past, and anon the noise of wings as sea fowls flew by.

Oh, Ocean, when thou choosest to smile, more beautiful thou art than flowery meadow plain!

He was haunted, though, by Pitt's words from the *Daedalus*: "It seems that the Admiralty has forgotten all about the king's little commission in the North Pacific."

He was, with all his other impetuosities, a loyal servant, of his country in any case, of the king if it came to that, and of the Admiralty, when it was necessary. Of the principle that besought perfection: totally, or as close to absolutely as was possible for a man in health and with purpose.

Vancouver looked at a young sailor with whole teeth in firm jaws, who was loosing the t'gallants and royals for the freshening breeze: am I mad?

So the work in the Sandwich Islands, it was not a part of his commission, but it was his duty as he saw it. He brought the Islands to peace by supporting the conquest and rule of Kamehama. Then he made the treaty for the cession of the Islands to Britain. He and the Hawaiian king sat upon the beach and agreed. We are now King George's people, said the native ruler.

The name George was as important to the commander as the name Joseph was a vexation. We are British people, said the king. Britain will protect you from the Yankees, said Vancouver. We desire to have an English ship here all the time, with one of your officers in its cabin, said the king. You will be a protectorate of the British Crown, which means that your government and your customs will not be abridged, said Vancouver. Let's dance, said Kamehama.

Now Vancouver saw the fore-topgallant yard pop

as the ship was slapped into the path of the trade wind, and he said: I do not think I am mad.

But he thought: if the Admiralty is too much caught up in their traditional war against the French, they will have forgotton all about my little commission, and they will not keep my promise of protection to the Islanders, and those people will fall to the energy of the rum running Yankees, as sure, as *they* would say, as shooting.

Damn the great naval thinkers who only dust their wigs and hang their overcoats in the closets at Whitehall! Damn their cosy vicinage! Vancouver, on the last few days of his survey, named places after Lavinia, Augusta, Sophia, Amelia, and Mary.

On the day that he announced their going home a lad who could climb ropes like a monkey but could not swim any better than one fell out of a boat and drowned. He was only the fourth fatality of the expedition. Most captains lost ten times as many as Vancouver had. Still he wished that this boy could have seen his native Stoke again. He wondered whether he would ever come round to looking forward to the sight of his native King's Lynn.

He watched another nonswimming fellow as he sprang easily from the bobstays to the bowsprit. Damn! If I am mad I am returning by this command to the madhouse.

At Friendly Cove two natives were hanging out nets to be dried and greased.

"I liked that Bam Goober fellow pretty well. In fact I think I liked him best of all the *Mamathni*," said the first Indian. "But you understand, they are still the white men. I am like my people . . ."

"A full man of the tribe," said the second Indian.

"Urinate on yourself. I agree with my people that we must pray that the day will come soon that all the white people go back to their home."

"In the sun?" asked the second Indian.

"May a bear defecate on your ear while you sleep, old man."

"I liked the man who drew images of the plants," said the second Indian.

"I liked that chief, Bam Goober. He was straight and tall . . ."

"He wasn't tall."

"He stood up straight, and he was always looking at things so hard that they could not hide anything from him that he wanted to know."

"I thought you were an artist," said the second Indian. "An artist is one who says things more simply than that. An artist puts white paint next to red paint so that one cannot help seeing the red paint."

"I will tell you that it seems as silly to me as to you that I thought the *Mamathni* were gods," said the younger man. "But that Bam Goober was close to being a god. He lacked one quality that would have made him a god."

"What is that?" asked his teacher.

"He looked so hard at things that one might think he was mad. But he had no madness in him, none at all."

56

Captain Vancouver was doubled over with pain in his chest and stomach, coughing, and fighting for breath. It was as if he had a Haida spear in him, as if he had been shot by a French musket. All for ten shillings a day.

They had sped by the coast of Peru as fast as the trades would take them. All the while he remained below decks, bent over his table, looking at the large scale map. The men in his boats had nosed along the littoral for ten thousand miles, and now there was a clear British picture of the farthest coast from the simple tropic to the contorted Arctic. Before they saw home again they would have voyaged sixty-five thousand English miles, ten thousand more than the epic commission of the *Resolution*. Yet they had been supplied only twice by the *Daedalus*. The *Discovery* was a rotting, stinking hulk as it creaked past the coastline of Peru and headed for refitting and repairs at Valparaiso, permission coming from Santiago.

Santiago. There was a saint for you. He could not have appeared at a better time. He lay in his sheets and stuffed the corner of the bolster into his mouth, trying to stay the coughing. He left a pink smear on the cotton. The coast from California north continues to become more complicated all the time, till one can only guess at the rivers of ice. He had said to James Cook that the glaciers were rivers of ice. The chunks of ice banged against the hull as they lay in Cook's River during ebb tide, and the chunks of ice banged against the hull again as they lay in Cook's Inlet during the flood. The Spaniards did not publish their charts because they coveted the dream of secrecy. But the coast is there, under California sun or behind New Norfolk mist. So his charts would be there as well, fact now by perseverance, equal to the real. His men had made a quarter million soundings that would be recorded for the eyes of a million sailors. If strangers were to come from the sun they could scan these hard-won facts and journey wide of peril. It had been phenomenally long and hard labour, and if the Admiralty had forgotten them heaven had not, and if there were no heaven, then the future would look with equal daylight sense at the coast of rock and sand, and the *Discovery's* map upon the wall. On the way from Monterey to Valparaiso he touched up the maps of Mexico a little. He wanted to get out in the boats there, but even in that warm sea his lungs contracted and he leaned over hard to find breath. The leaning futtock shrouds mocked him and he designed to stand up straight and walk with moderate speed, which he managed, bringing pain and dizziness and a bad temperament.

Every time they encountered an uninhabited island off the coast of South America he despatched a boat whose crew would plant vegetable seeds for future Crusoes. Menzies always went ashore with them for the opposite reason. His original horticultural section of the deck had trebled in area, and now that the great survey was officially at an end, he seemed to feel that his own project was the ship's only reason for staying afloat. It required that any passing pedestrian must look carefully on his way rather than moving through the passage of his memory. On one occasion a midshipman knocked a pot with a small spruce in it to the deck, and Menzies went into a tempestuous Scottish dance while he yelled at the confused young man, and bent to reinsert in its soil the alien young tree.

They passed on this course their fourth Christmas away from Britian, and while the men were inured to the whims and designs and fancies of their superiors, some of the officers allowed their impatience to be aired. Mr. Puget especially was a leading spokesman of the hurried faction.

"The sooner I can see myself surrounded by English faces I do not recognize, the sooner will fade from my memory the crowd of brown faces notable for nothing more salubrious than their uncomprehending stupidity," was the way he put his eagerness to see his native heath again.

In return, though some days later, Vancouver passed a less than enthusiastic remark about the manner in which Mr. Puget handled the sailing of the *Chatham*.

They spent a good portion of the southern summer in Chile, replacing the rotten masts, furnishing new lines and anchors, filling the water casks, boiling up a few tons of sauerkraut, and repairing the intestines and gums of the one hundred and forty Britishers. All the while, Dr. Menzies kept a jealous eye on any activity near his greenery.

Vancouver reluctantly decided to seek the attention of the governor's own physician in Santiago, but this man only advised him to get plenty of bed rest and stay out of the rain. After the English captain had placed his hat squarely upon his large head and walked with all possible grace from the office, the doctor told his assistants that he had just seen a middle-aged man dying of consumption. Vancouver was almost thirty-seven.

He thought he might die on the mule that carried him back to Valparaiso. When he got back to the court and thence onto his ship, Menzies ordered him to his bed. There he lay trying to sleep in the middle of the afternoon. Presently the daily rain of summer announced itself upon the deck above, and as it beat heavily on the new planking, George Vancouver fell into sleep.

57

They leaned their way round the Horn in the last week of May, not the best of times: they fought against gales filled with hard snow, past great islands of ice as high as the maintop. But after four years in the Pacific, no prodigy of weather would prevent them from putting keel into the home ocean. The patched canvas and strapped spars protested but held, the clothing of the men was torn and rubbed through and the uniforms of the officers in worn and precarious condition, as the king's sloop *Discovery* drew fifteen feet of the Atlantic for the first time in four years and two months.

At St. Helena, Vancouver found that he was in an ocean of war, and his heart sped with anticipation. The British man-of-war, *Sceptre*, was just leaving the island with a train of merchant ships captured from the French and Dutch.

But he was told that the French government, in recognition of his great work that could not fail to benefit ships of all flags, had extended safe passage to the *Discovery* and the *Chatham*.

However, as Vancouver and his company were departing the governor's palace, he spied a Dutch merchantman just arrived in the harbour. Immediately he sent Mr. Johnstone aboard to seize it as a prize of war. It was not a very ennobling nor even exciting act of war, but it was nevertheless a military deed. Coughing and sucking for air almost constantly now, Vancouver had his men drilled in gunnery twice a day as soon as they had cleared the island's harbour. It was fine to resume the role of royal fighting ship, and it was a good sound, the reiterative explosions of the guns along both sides of this weathered old ship. The French safe passage was thus noisily abrogated.

Menzies, of course, had a fearful vision of a naval engagement resulting in damage to his collection of plants, nurtured so assiduously over four years, and the destruction or loss of his sketchbooks and journals, so much filled with data and descriptions of exotic flora and animals that could not have been transported through the weather. He found a way to approach Vancouver about his concern.

"Would it not be a shame, my captain, if all your intricate work over all these years, over all those thousands of miles, would it not be a catastrophe were a Frenchman's lucky cannon to lob a bomb into the middle of your chart room?"

Vancouver stood as straight as his scarred organs would allow.

"That, sir, would indeed be a fateful event that might be rued in a backward glance upon it. But it would not be avoided in the future by a patriot."

"You will understand, of course," said Menzies, "that as a civilian and a scientist, I cannot consider one of the navy's periodic squabbles with their French counterparts to be of importance equal to the information and *life* I seek to bring to the Royal Society."

"You may fuck the Royal Society!"

"I beg your pardon?"

Vancouver went into a coughing fit that continued beyond the point at which both men thought it would end, several times.

Then he said, "Mr. Menzies, those wild rhubarbs and cedar bushes will be growing out of the soil of New South Wales or Queen Charlotte's Islands a hundred years from this day. We naval persons sail fervently into battle with the ships of the regicide so that we might fairly expect the existence of a Great Britain a century hence. Do you understand my intention?"

Menzies thought of the long coughing spell that was now reinstituted, when he replied.

"Oh, yes, sir."

"Do not be insolent, surgeon. It is a dangerous attribute during a time of war."

Soon the *Discovery* overtook the halting convoy headed by Captain Essington of the *Sceptre*. This latter was not greatly impressed by the battle condition of the surveyor's ship, but he was happy to have some practical assistance in keeping the merchantmen from scattering all over the Atlantic.

So the *Discovery* joined the group, sometimes chasing a merchantman back toward the pack, sometimes raising a great din as her commander called for another training session with the guns.

Upon the first day of September, a few leagues north of the Azores, one of the civilian vessels ran up a flag of distress. The *Discovery*, which had had to haul in half her sail to keep to the slow pace of the convoy, easily caught up to the unhappy vessel and saw that she was lying deep in the swells, her decks awash. She might be able to stay afloat, but she would be no longer able to sail with the other ships, even though some of them were themselves disabled. There was nothing to be done but to set her aflame and abandon her to the middle of the grey ocean.

Vancouver despatched his yawl to see to the job.

The crew of the doomed ship got aboard and left as the flames leapt up greased riggings and across decks. Soon the yawl was alongside the *Discovery*, and the men were yanking themselves up the rocking side of the ship. Now blocks were dropped and the yawl began its ascent, but at that moment a monstrous wave clapped the boat against the side, and the shattered pieces tumbled one by one into the tangled sea.

Vancouver held his breath and stood with firm feet on the heaving quarterdeck. In a moment the first tears he had allowed past his eyeballs in three decades mingled with wind-blown sea water on the decrepit skin of his cheek. As he turned to go to his cabin he caught the eye of Menzies, who had been watching him from the low doorway of his makeshift greenhouse.

It was at least his second great loss of the voyage. It would have taken several years just to imagine the places to which that little boat had taken the surveyors. In the cabin he sat by his writing desk and inscribed his deep feelings for the second time during the expedition:

> I do not recollect that my feelings ever suffered so much on any occasion of a similar nature, as at that moment. The cutter was the boat I had constantly used; in her I had travelled very many miles; in her I had repeatedly escaped from danger; she had always brought me safely home; and although she was but an inanimate conveniency, to which, it may possibly be thought, no affection could be attached, yet I felt myself under such an obligation for her services, that when she was dashed to pieces before my eyes an involuntary emotion suddenly seized my breast, and I was compelled to turn away to hide a weakness (for which though my own gratitude might find an

apology) I should have thought improper to have publicly manifested.

Then he blotted the ink and wept upon the blotter, wept for the little boat he called she, wept for James Cook, wept for Don Juan, wept out of exhaustion and destroyed hope, and finally allowed himself to weep for George Vancouver, utterly and perfectly now alone.

58

If only Archibald Menzies had been an officer of the Royal Navy, things would have gone a lot more smoothly though with a like acrimony.

It was in accordance with naval directions that Captain Vancouver called in all the officers' journals for the four-and-a-half-year voyage. Mr. Mudge and Mr. Baker handed over their thick journals with brisk cheer. Mr. Puget was a little reluctant to exhibit his rather thin accomplishment. Whidbey stayed to scribble some last lines to his thousands of pages and then delivered his masterwork, in three trips.

Mr. Menzies announced that he would be obliged to retain his journal.

"I hope that after more than four years at sea, and sixty-five thousand miles sailed thereon, it has been impressed upon your brain that I am legally and royally commissioned captain of the *Discovery*," said Vancouver, his face red not so much from anger as from the furies disporting in his blood.

"It would have been difficult to remain ignorant of that," allowed the botanist.

"It is my hope also that it has not escaped your attention that your place of sleep has for that same period been the same H.M.S. *Discovery*."

"Aye, and a well-run ship she has been," said Menzies.

Who could tell whether he were mocking the notion that he was simply another sailor under the Flag, or announcing the Scottishness that seemed to pique the captain's temperament?

"Where did you attain your schooling, sir?"

"At Wrem Parish School, where one learns principally to behave, and then with more curiosity and individual attendance at the Royal Botanic Garden, and the Medical College both in Edinburgh."

"Yes, Edinburgh. Well, even in Edinburgh, I suppose, your betters taught you something of logic?"

"My betters were not at school; but I did, I will agree, learn much in the way of logic whilst I was there. I have found that logic is an excellent device against sickness," said Menzies, looking significantly at the various features of Vancouver's face.

Vancouver stood up to his gaze. He could feel his own strength as if it were another's that did not fit. He felt like a sack that will fold and topple inward when one more handful of beans is removed from it.

"Then please strain your fine Edinburgh mind to this, sir," he said. "The Admiralty, which is the ultimate earthly power over this vessel and its mission, has instructed me to gather all the journals kept by the gentlemen who have travelled upon her planks to the Pacific North West. You, sir, were in her contingent."

Menzies caught Zach. Mudge's eye and saw his friend's amusement through a blue cloud of fresh pipe smoke. There was, in fact, a numerous crowd to be noticed now, witnessing the latest confrontation between navy and Royal Society.

"Captain, I know not what matters are recorded by your uniformed officers in their journals, but I assume that they are mainly concerns military and nautical, and quite familiar in their form and useful in their content to your omnipotent Admiralty. My journal, meanwhile, is replete with drawings and descriptions of what you have generally been contented to term weeds. They would prove to be but the most tiresome of data to your superiors moored to their offices in the grand city. But the material in question is of considerable interest to the Royal Society, and to the king's gardener at Kew. You see, I can drop the royal reference as well as the next man."

"The fact remains," said Vancouver, "that I have been instructed by the Admiralty to receive your journal, whether it be filled with cowslips or poetry."

"Just so, I have been ordered by Mr. Joseph Banks . . ."

"That Goddamned meddling fool!"

" . . . to hand my journals and sketches to the secretary of state for home affairs."

Vancouver turned and walked away, in a show of absolute anger, but really because he had to be alone in his cabin when the coughing fit came. It came and blood came with it. After the pain had allowed him to open his eyes, he took out his pen and ink and wrote a formal request that Dr. Menzies hand over to him all the journals he had written while under his command. He had the letter delivered to Menzies by the hand of Mr. Whidbey.

"Why don't you accede to the Old Man's fancy and let him have your jottings?" this temperate man suggested. "You will be afforded the opportunity, once ashore, to retrieve them for your Mr. Banks."

"The nature of my vocation, plus the nature of my person, marry, and come to this," replied Archibald Menzies, "that I do not accede to fancy."

Whereupon saying, he gave Mr. Whidbey his sick book.

"This you may take to your captain. I acted for

him as surgeon, first in secret doing all the work of that drunken quack Cranstoun, and then when he drank himself into oblivion, doing the job in the open. Take him this surgeon's record and tell him I have thus fulfilled my obligation to his command."

Vancouver did not refuse to accept this book with his name lately so prominent in it. It did, after all, constitute a body of facts, which it was his responsibility to shepherd home.

But he conveyed another written message to Menzies. From this one the botanist learned that he was under arrest, that as a gentleman he had the freedom of the ship, but that upon their tying to at Shannon, he should deliver himself to the naval authority, there to be constrained until charges might be officially read and a court appointed.

59

Did a man who was under arrest yet act in his free man's profession? Did Menzies yet call upon Captain Vancouver, pronounce upon his health, and order him about, as a physician is expected to do in his traditional imperious way?

Vancouver solved that problem, if indeed it was one, by keeping away from Dr. Menzies.

But Mr. Menzies was also a naturalist, and so did not bedevil himself with such hypothetical enquiry. He spent near all his waking time around his greenhouse, sprinkling and thinning and poking, giving all his physician's care to the miniature earth's garden in his care.

A good number of his specimens, it has been mentioned, were under glass. But as the numbers had grown, the little arborium had sprawled out in every direction, and climbed above the height of a man, and the glass long since exhausted, Menzies had worked out a system of tarpaulins to be stretched over the plants during times of equatorial rains or high seas. After many arguments and snide remarks, he had been extended the services of a seaman, whose job it was to attend the tarpaulin in question, and also to repair any occasional damage that might befall the pots or frames during the normal course of seafaring and weather and work about the vessel. We have seen that the spreading of Menzies' sphere of interest had caused displeasure to the ship's captain, and indeed there were occasions upon which a sailor in the course of his regular duty might step from a lanyard and put his heel through the corner of a seedling box.

A few days after the *Discovery* had joined the convoy, Menzies went aboard the *Sceptre* to discuss matters pharmaceutical with her ship's doctor, an old friend from medical college. While he was thus away from his own charge, a Dutch sail was spotted to the east, and there was therefore no transportation permitted between ships, as the *Discovery* and Mr. Essington's crew took up their much rehearsed battle positions.

But before the enemy bark could close with them, an Atlantic squall did, and the English vessels had all they could do to keep the convoy from crashing itself to bits or dispersing about the wild grey sea. Rain cut cold and sharp into Menzies' face as he endeavoured to catch a glimpse of his own ship to no avail. The hard but uncertain wind kept seizing the ships from the stern and trying to spin them to their doom. This nasty storm continued all night and till past noon the following day, and was succeeded by a drenching downpour falling through quite still air. There was, of course, no sign of the Lowlands' man-of-war.

In the unpleasant September rain, Menzies bullied some sailors into transporting him by way of a skiff to his own ship. He had a foreboding that was fed by nearly half a decade of difficult husbandry: he had a desperate and foolish hope that he would see his gentle seedlings and shoots and pygmy trees yet living and hale.

He might as well have expected a George Vancouver in the pink of good health.

What he saw broke his heart. He held his breath and stood with firm feet upon the slanting deck. The hundreds of plants that should have been under tarpaulin were strewn about the deck, or remained only sodden stumps in the mud. Four and a half years of toil and promises were gone in a night one week from home. Many of the glass windows were smashed, and the inhabitants below, born and nourished in placid Polynesian sunshine, now dashed to the deck and half covered in mud by the mean autumn rains of the North Atlantic. The guard was, of course, nowhere in sight.

"We are an unfortunate pair this week," said George Vancouver. "First I lose the cutter, and then you lose your posies."

It did not look to the naturalist as if the litter of broken glass could have been caused by rain and wind.

"Where is my guard?" shouted the furious Menzies. "I want him punished. I want him to receive twelve dozen lashes, and I want him hauled below the keel."

Vancouver laughed, and then he coughed.

"Do not allow yourself to descend into hysteria, Dr. Menzies, for it does not become you in the least. Recall that you yourself are under arrest and hardly in a position to call for an enlisted man's punishment. In fact, you had no business, being arrested, in leaving my ship."

"Then I will settle things for that man myself," Menzies cried. "Where is he?"

"You are shouting, man of science. I am amazed. As for your man, blame him not. During the threat of a possible Dutch enounter, he was called away to more pressing military duty."

Menzies guffawed.

"Oh yes, you and your military duty! You're no more a man of war, you popinjay! You are a passable explorer, but you are a fool who dream of dunking the Armada!"

Vancouver's face turned a red-purple. He began to shout as loudly as did Menzies.

"You are insolent and contemptuous, sir! I have been too liberal in allowing you a gentleman's arrest. You will be confined to your quarters where you will be outfitted with irons upon your foot and your hands, you son-of-a-bitch porridge-eating Scotch lamb-fucker!"

"Mayhap 'twould be better were I a lisping Peruvian gentleman with lace coming out my nether hole?"

Vancouver began to scream obscene and cruel words into the rain, and neither man noticed the crowd of officers and enlisted men who kept their distance as by accord long reached. Vancouver had been wearing his sword since they had left St. Helena. Now he drew it, and as he alternately screamed and coughed in the rain, he began to smash the remaining windows of the greenhouse. His language was a wonder and a horror, coming out of this man whose decorum for a quarter century at sea had been equalled by no other officer.

Menzies stood and watched for a while. He knew the names, Latin and English, that had been bestowed by his predecessors or himself upon each green victim. He knew the chemical composition of the soil around each root. The people who were watching the affray knew all at once that he was gone. Soon he was back, and he had with him his long-unseen Daniel Thiermay flintlock.

Vancouver looked at him and laughed, and kicked a potted plant across the planking toward its caretaker.

Would the venerable French pistol work in the rain? Why did the officers stand and watch? Menzies aimed and squeezed and there was a little flash but that was all. Vancouver shouted and cursed, and when Peter Puget looked to set his foot on the steps leading up to that deck, Vancouver threatened him with his blade.

Menzies held the weapon under his rain cape and shook out more powder.

"Will you want me round your neck till I fall?" shouted Vancouver.

Menzies lifted the flintlock and aimed it a second time at the captain of the *Discovery*. Vancouver looked directly at him, and began to cough. He coughed and coughed again trying not to bend over. Menzies squeezed, and this time the shot sped through the rain and into the breast of the coughing man.

Vancouver plunged backward a step and down upon one knee, and now he was coughing blood onto the broad lapels of his uniform. He collapsed onto his side, and his hand reached for the rail. Menzies held the pistol by his side and watched as Vancouver pulled himself to his feet, and then full of pain, leaned upon the rail. A gust of wind punched into the mainsail, and every man took a little shuffling step to stay erect, save their captain who seemed to be lifted by some strength unwitnessed, over the rail and into the unsolicitous sea.

George Bowering

George Bowering is a major figure in Canadian literature. He has published many books of poetry, literary criticism, and other prose. He won the 1969 Governor General of Canada's Award for poetry with his two books, *Rocky Mountain Foot* and *The Gangs of Kosmos*.

Bowering grew up in the Okanagan Valley in central British Columbia, among fruit orchards and mountains. He now lives with his wife and daughter in Vancouver where he pursues his hobbies: fastball, and collecting frogs, T-shirts, and sneakers.

His interest in his namesake began many years ago and he has published both a radio play and a long poem on George Vancouver.

Burning Water is Bowering's first full-length novel since 1967.